"I need a man."

Heat penetrated Kate's cheeks. "I mean, I want to hire one of your escorts."

She glanced over at the man on the other side of the room, then did a double take. He fit all her specifications, with a few she hadn't thought of. He was tall, with stylishly cut dark hair, clear blue eyes and a sensual mouth. He was handsome enough to be a movie star. He had broad shoulders narrowing to slim hips, and his custom-made suit enhanced every detail of his powerful build.

An added bonus was the air of authority he radiated. No one would ever guess this man was rented for the evening. She wondered fleetingly why he was doing this kind of work. But it didn't matter. He was absolutely perfect for her purpose.

"I'll take *him*."

Dear Reader,

Welcome to the Silhouette **Special Edition** experience! With your search for consistently satisfying reading in mind, every month the authors and editors of Silhouette **Special Edition** aim to offer you a stimulating blend of deep emotions and high romance.

The name Silhouette **Special Edition** and the distinctive arch on the cover represent a commitment—a commitment to bring you six sensitive, substantial novels each month. In the pages of a Silhouette **Special Edition**, compelling true-to-life characters face riveting emotional issues—and come out winners. All the authors in the series strive for depth, vividness and warmth in writing these stories of living and loving in today's world.

The result, we hope, is romance you can believe in. Deeply emotional, richly romantic, infinitely rewarding—that's the Silhouette **Special Edition** experience. Come share it with us—six times a month!

From all the authors and editors of Silhouette **Special Edition**,

Best wishes,

Leslie Kazanjian,
Senior Editor

TRACY SINCLAIR
The Girl Most Likely To

Silhouette Special Edition

Published by Silhouette Books New York

America's Publisher of Contemporary Romance

Books by Tracy Sinclair

TRACY SINCLAIR

Author of more than twenty-five Silhouette novels, Tracy Sinclair also contributes to various magazines and newspapers. She says her years as a photojournalist provided the most exciting adventures—and misadventures—of her life. An extensive traveler—from Alaska to South America, and most places in between—and a dedicated volunteer worker—from suicide-prevention programs to English-as-a-second-language lessons—the California resident has accumulated countless fascinating experiences, settings and acquaintances to draw on in plotting her romances.

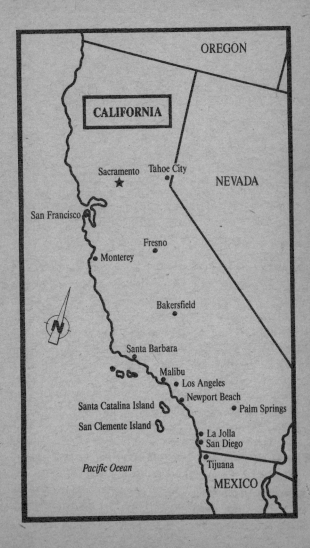

Chapter One

Kate Beaumont opened her mail indifferently when she got home from work that night. It seldom contained anything more interesting than a brochure for a glamorous cruise she didn't have time to take.

She tossed most of the catalogues and advertisements in the wastebasket, and left some of the more obvious junk mail unopened. A long white envelope almost followed the rest—until she noticed the return address. Hollywood High School Reunion Committee.

Kate's hazel eyes were pensive as she removed the single sheet of paper and read the bold black print across the top: COME ONE, COME ALL TO THE 10-YEAR RE-UNION OF THE CLASS OF '80.

Had it been that long since graduation? In some ways it seemed incredible, yet so much had happened since then. The long years of college, then the struggle to be taken seriously in the field of science, where youth was considered an affliction and women were often regarded as an intrusion into a man's world.

She dismissed the ongoing problem and began to read the letter. It gave details of the dinner dance that would be held at a Los Angeles hotel. All alumni were urged to attend with their spouses or current love interest, although it wasn't put in those words. The date was only a week and a half away.

A handwritten note at the bottom of the page explained the short notice. It was from Pat Barsky, the coordinator of the reunion. "Sorry your name slipped through the cracks somehow. That's what happens when you depend on volunteers. Hope you can still make it."

Kate wasn't surprised at being overlooked. It was the story of her high-school years. While all the other girls were going to football games and school dances, she'd held down a part-time job and spent the rest of her free time studying so she could qualify for a college scholarship. The only people who took any notice of Kate were the teachers.

Palmer Wesley, the campus football hero, would have been amused to know she had a wild crush on him. His girlfriend was Betty Livingston, head cheerleader, homecoming queen, most popular girl in the senior class.

Did Palmer and Betty get married as everyone predicted? And what became of Estelle Washburn, who drove a red convertible, and Farley Thomas, whose father was somebody big in the movie studios?

As Kate remembered long-forgotten classmates, she felt a stirring of excitement. It would be fun to see what they had done with their lives, especially since she could finally match their accomplishments. It might be a very stimulating evening, now that they were all adults with their priorities straight.

The sparkle in Kate's eyes died as she reread the letter. How could she go without an escort? The trendiest clothes and membership in the best sorority might not matter any longer, but the world still had a mind-set that went back to Noah's ark. A woman who wasn't married, engaged or seriously involved with a man was an object of pity. Kate was damned if she was going to be patronized at this stage by her peers. No, she'd just have to forego the reunion.

Tossing the letter in the wastebasket, she went into the kitchen to put a TV dinner in the microwave. But while she waited for the bell to ring, Kate's resentment rose. Why should she be too uncomfortable to attend because of other people's close-minded beliefs? She could go to the reunion with an ax murderer and be accepted, as long as he was presentable. It wasn't fair!

More than she'd ever wanted anything in life, Kate wished for the perfect date to accompany her to the reunion. Someone tall, dark and handsome, with a physique so gorgeous even Palmer Wesley would be impressed.

Even as her imagination soared, Kate realized how futile her dreams were. Only a fairy godmother could grant them. The kind of man she was looking for existed only in magazine ads. Her mouth curved sardonically. Maybe she should go to an agency and hire one.

Kate paused in the act of slipping on an oven mitt. That wasn't such a wild idea. Weren't there escort services for men *and* women? The people they supplied had to be attractive. The evening newspaper was on the kitchen table. She turned to the classified section and found what she was looking for.

Half of one column was devoted to escort bureaus, each proclaiming its superiority. The extravagant prose made Kate's eyebrows climb. Agencies with names like Fun For All and A Little Night Magic promised unlimited pleasure. "Why stay home alone?" one asked. "Our discreet, experienced escorts can fulfill all your fantasies." Kate's shoulders slumped as she sat back in her chair. Well, another good idea shot down. These places were offering more than she required.

As she picked at the unappetizing TV dinner, her eyes kept straying back to the newspaper. Maybe she was being hasty. While it was true that some of those firms were undoubtedly shady, some might not be. Besides, she didn't have to avail herself of any of their more lurid services.

Kate made up her mind abruptly. She didn't intend to sit at home feeling sorry for herself like Cinderella. Who needed a fairy godmother? She was perfectly capable of handling her own life.

Her decision had seemed sensible the night before, but Kate was having second thoughts the next morning when she walked past the address written on the scrap of paper clutched in her moist hand.

Top Hat Escort Service had the most low-key ad in the newspaper. That what why she'd chosen it. But the neighborhood was slightly seedy, and the office building matched its surroundings. Kate wouldn't have been reassured if she'd heard the conversation between the two men in the escort bureau upstairs.

They were about the same age and seemed to be friends rather than business associates. Although they were presently having a mild disagreement, Garrett Richmond was sprawled in a chair, his long legs stretched out and crossed at the ankles. The casual pose didn't lessen the disapproval on his rugged face as he gazed at the man sitting behind the scarred desk.

"When are you going to give up these crazy get-rich-quick schemes and get into something legitimate?"

Foster Gray grinned. "You sound like my mother."

"She has my sympathies. Parents have a right to expect their children to be grown up by the time they're thirty-four."

"What more adult business could I be in?" Foster chuckled.

Garrett's eyes narrowed. "I trust that doesn't mean what it sounds like."

"Hey! I provide a legitimate service."

"I hope so. I've pulled you out of a lot of scrapes, but my patience has limits."

"Would I lie to my old college buddy? This type of thing might seem tacky to you, but not all of us have a family business to step into." Under Foster's geniality was a touch of rancor.

"I told you I'd give you a job any time you wanted one."

"In the menswear department selling neckties?" Foster asked derisively.

"We don't have an opening for a vice president without any retail experience," Garrett drawled.

"Is this where I get the pep talk again? The one about working my way up to be manager of one of your department stores?"

"You could do worse. I plan to open three more in the near future. You could be my right-hand man, if you proved yourself."

Foster shook his head. "A nine-to-five job with a carrot in front of my nose isn't my speed. I want it all, and I want it now."

Before Garrett could answer, the door opened and Kate entered the office. After an agonizing period of indecision, she'd stuck to her original plan.

The shabby office didn't inspire confidence, but the man behind the desk seemed respectable. He had a pleasant face, not quite handsome but nice-looking. His sport jacket and neat tie gave further reassurance. She didn't glance at the other man in the room.

"Good morning, can I help you?" Foster smiled at her.

"Well, I, uh..."

Kate had expected a receptionist. Having to explain her requirement in front of two men was embarrassing. She clutched her purse and swallowed hard, trying to regain her poise. After all, she was there on a perfectly legitimate errand.

From his vantage point in the corner, Garrett inspected Kate with interest. She didn't seem like the sort of woman who would pay for an escort. About twenty-seven or twenty-eight, he decided, with a good figure, although it was difficult to tell. The no-nonsense navy suit had a calf-length skirt, and her high-necked white blouse concealed any curves that might be underneath. Her legs were slim, however, what he could see of them, with trim ankles and dainty feet.

In that prim outfit she was rather colorless, although her skin was flawless and her eyes were a tawny gold. Maybe if she wore more makeup. Good bone structure and delicate features went unnoticed. With her long hair strained back and the palest of pink lipstick outlining a generous mouth, she looked like the old stereotype of a spinster schoolteacher.

Or someone masquerading as one? Garrett decided against the notion because of her nervousness. This was clearly a woman who was doing something she considered daring. Her vulnerability touched Garrett.

"What can I do for you?" Foster prodded, when Kate had trouble stating her business.

"I need a man." Swift heat deepened the color in her already rosy cheeks. "I mean, I want to hire one of your escorts for one night a week from Saturday."

"That can certainly be arranged," Foster answered soothingly.

"It's for my high-school reunion. Everyone else will be bringing someone, and I don't have—that is, I'm not going with anyone at the moment."

Kate was furious with herself. Why was she telling this man her life story? It didn't concern him. This was strictly a business transaction.

"We'll be happy to supply you with an escort, Miss...?" Foster looked at her questioningly.

"Kate Beaumont."

"It's a pleasure to be of service, Miss Beaumont." He quoted her a price before asking, "How would you like to pay?"

"I'll give you a check." She looked at him uncertainly. "But don't I get to pick one out?"

"I can show you some photos."

As Foster opened a drawer, Garrett stood up, frowning. "Can I speak to you for a minute, Foster?"

Kate glanced at him automatically, then did a double take. The man fit all her specifications, with a few she hadn't thought of. He was tall, perhaps six foot two, had dark hair stylishly cut and was handsome enough to be a movie star. A straight nose, sensual mouth and clear blue eyes, deep-set in a fringe of spiky lashes, made his face a memorable one.

His physique was superior, like the rest of him. Even Palmer hadn't been built in that elongated triangle of broad shoulders narrowing to slim hips and long, muscular legs. His custom-made suit enhanced every detail of the man's powerful build.

An added bonus was the air of authority he radiated. No one would ever guess this man was rented for the evening. Kate wondered fleetingly why he was doing this kind of work, but she dismissed the conjecture. It didn't matter. He was absolutely perfect for her purpose.

"You can look at these photos." Foster spread some eight-by-ten glossies on the desk. "I'm sure you'll find someone here to satisfy you."

"That won't be necessary. I'll take *him*." Kate had the grace to realize how abrupt that must sound. "I'm sorry," she said to Garrett. "I meant I'd like to engage your services, if you're available."

Foster started to laugh. "I don't think you could afford to pay for his time."

"You've already quoted the lady a price." Garrett extended his hand to Kate. "Garrett Richmond. I'd be very happy to escort you to your reunion."

"You have to be kidding!" Foster stared at him, openmouthed.

"I don't believe you have any other engagements for me that night," Garrett said evenly.

"Well, no." Foster looked at his friend with obvious disbelief.

"Right. Then I'll see you on the seventeenth, Miss Beaumont. Mr. Gray will supply me with details about time and place." Garrett left the office after an exchanged glance with Foster.

Kate knew something was wrong, but she didn't know what. Was Garrett usually assigned to the women who wanted more than an escort? That would account for his higher price. He would be worth it. For one burning instant she let herself imagine what it would be like to lie in Garrett's arms, to feel every hard angle of that magnificent body making an impression on her yielding flesh.

"You can make out the check to Top Hat Escort Service." Foster broke the spell.

"I have my checkbook right here," she said breathlessly.

He accepted the slip of paper, gazing at her with a slight smile. "I know you'll be satisfied with your choice, Miss Beaumont."

Kate's anticipation mounted as the date of the reunion neared. She was tempted to buy a new dress for the occasion, then decided against it. Her present wardrobe was sufficient for her limited social life. Anything truly smashing would be a waste of money, and Garrett was already costing a fortune, even at regular rates. She didn't regret her decision, though. He was going to be worth every penny.

Excitement raced through Kate as she dressed for the big event. Her cheeks were becomingly flushed, and her eyes sparkled as she applied her customary pale pink lipstick.

After brushing her hair until it crackled, she thought about trying a new hairdo. It was a good idea that didn't work. The thick mass of light brown hair refused to stay anchored on top of her head, and she couldn't think of anything else to do with it. Finally she gave up and clipped it back with the usual barrette.

The dress she'd decided on was a two-piece black silk jersey with long sleeves and a high, round neck. The saleswoman had said it would be appropriate anywhere.

Maybe for someone who wanted to be indistinguishable in a crowd. Kate looked in the mirror with dissatisfaction. She would have changed, if she'd had anything more glamorous to wear. The beige silk? It was equally conservative. The doorbell put an end to her indecision. Garrett had arrived.

He was even more handsome than she remembered. Or maybe it was the elegant dark suit and the snowy white linen shirt that emphasized his deep tan. Kate stood in the open doorway staring at him without returning his greeting.

Garrett gazed back at her, noticing how the black dress clung to her curved body. His original surmise was correct. She had a terrific figure. With a little makeup and her hair free of that damn clip, she'd be something special.

"May I come in?" he asked finally.

"Oh, I...of course. I should have—" She stopped and took a deep breath. "Forgive my nervousness. As you've probably guessed, I've never done this before. Hired someone to take me out, I mean. Not that there's anything wrong with what you do," she added hurriedly, afraid she'd sounded critical.

"Why don't we sit down and get acquainted?" he asked gently.

She looked at him doubtfully. "I guess we should leave."

Garrett consulted a thin gold watch on his wrist. "We have a little time yet, and we need to find out a few things about each other. I gather you want people to think we're going together."

"If you don't mind."

His smile made her pulse quicken. "It will be my pleasure."

"You don't have to overdo it. Just pretend we go out together a lot."

"You don't want me to give the impression that we're in love?"

Kate uttered a harsh laugh. "It's going to be hard enough to convince them that you'd even date someone like me."

He gazed at her impassively, not allowing his compassion to show. "Why would you say a thing like that? You're a very attractive woman."

"I think we'd better understand each other right now, Mr. Richmond. I don't know what your other clients expect, but all I require is an escort for the evening. Phony flattery isn't necessary."

"You don't think you're attractive?"

"What I think isn't important," she answered curtly. "Shall we go?"

"We haven't decided on a story yet. If we want to appear convincing, we'd better get our act together. Your friends are bound to ask questions, probably starting with where we met. What about at work?" He grinned suddenly. "I mean yours, not mine."

She shook her head. "You don't look like a scientist."

"Is that what you are?"

"I'm a microbiologist. I work for the Strawbridge Research Institute."

"That's very impressive." He smiled engagingly. "At the risk of sounding like a male chauvinist, which I'm not, you don't look like a scientist, either."

"A lot of people have trouble believing it," she said dryly. "As far back as high school everybody snickered when I said I wanted to do research work."

"I don't know why. Women can be anything they choose these days."

"But they usually choose something more glamorous when they're young. In high school almost every girl's ambition is to be a cheerleader."

"That didn't appeal to you?"

"I wouldn't have had time, even if I'd stood a chance. I worked after school every day to get money for college. I never took part in any school activities."

"That's too bad," he said gently.

Kate lifted her chin. "You don't have to feel sorry for me. It was worth it. I have an interesting career in my chosen field. I wonder how many of my classmates can say the same?"

"Haven't you kept in touch with any of them?"

"I didn't have many friends in high school. My only really close friend moved to Boston. She doesn't know any more about the people in our class than I do." After a pause Kate said, "You're probably wondering why I'm even bothering to go tonight."

Garrett smiled. "I can guess. Curiosity to see if the campus queen got fat or the student-body president lost his hair."

Kate felt her tension relax. Garrett was very easy to talk to, and it was nice to confide in someone she'd never see again. She could air all her frustrations without worrying about being embarrassed at some later date.

Returning his smile she said, "You're partly right, but it's the head cheerleader and the captain of the football team. I was hopelessly in love with Palmer Wesley, who was, of course, in love with Betty Livingston. She was everything I wanted to be—pretty, popular, the girl voted most likely to succeed. Remember those predictions they used to print below your name in the yearbook? Under mine it said, the girl most likely to finish college."

"That's not so bad."

"No. They really had to hunt for something to say, but I guess it could have been worse. They could have said most likely to have to hire someone to take her to her reunion."

Kate's bravado so obviously covered pain that Garrett's heart twisted. He was touched by the picture he was getting of a lonely, insecure young girl. She'd had enough courage and tenacity to stick to her goals, but the price had been high. Early experiences could shape a person's vision of herself. Too bad Kate didn't realize what personal potential she had. Garrett found himself wanting to give her the assurance she lacked.

"You're not the only woman who finds herself between men when a big occasion arises," he told her. "I admire your initiative."

"I lucked out with you," she said frankly. "When my former classmates get a glimpse of you, maybe they'll stop thinking of me as poor, little mousy Kate Beaumont."

"I don't know what you looked like in high school, but you're certainly not mousy now. And that isn't a phony compliment."

She tried not to show her pleasure at the warmth in his voice. "You must admit I'm not the glamorous type."

"You could be, if that's what you wanted." He tilted his head to look at her consideringly. "You have good features and beautiful skin. You also have one hell of a body. I don't know why you cover it up so completely."

Her color deepened as his eyes appraised her figure with male expertise. "I'm not interested in calling attention to myself," she stated primly.

"You are tonight."

"Well, maybe," she admitted.

"Then may I suggest you take that godawful clip off your hair and turn your skirt up at the waist. You have beautiful legs. Show them off."

"I'd feel silly," she protested.

"Try it and then decide."

Before she could stop him, Garrett unclipped her barrette. His long fingers combed through her hair, spreading it over her shoulders. His nearness and the intimate touch of his hands struck her dumb. She stared up at him, feeling an unfamiliar throbbing deep inside.

"That's much better. Now the skirt. Turn it up," he ordered.

Kate did as he said, afraid Garrett might do it for her.

"More than that," he instructed.

After she'd folded the waistband over several times he stood back for a critical appraisal. A look of satisfaction crossed his face.

"Much better. Do you have any earrings?"

"A couple of pairs," she said, wondering why she was allowing this.

Garrett wasn't impressed by the scant contents of her jewelry box. "I know of a department store that stays open until nine. We'll stop and get something suitable."

Kate tried to reestablish control. "A pair of earrings isn't going to change me into a femme fatale."

"You're already on your way." He put his hands on her shoulders and guided her to the full-length mirror on the closet door.

Kate stared at a stranger. The woman in the mirror had long, tumbled hair that looked as though a man had ruffled it while kissing her. She wore a figure-flattering dress that was very provocative. The short skirt revealed long, slender legs that promised an equally enticing body.

"I don't believe it," she whispered.

"Trust me." Garrett glanced at his watch. "Come on, we'll have to hustle if we're going to make a stop."

Kate would have expected Garrett to drive a sports car, but not a Ferrari. They cost a fortune. His rates must be astronomical—unless grateful women gave him gifts. She didn't want to pursue the thought. Garrett had too much potential to squander it like that.

He drove swiftly, yet competently to a mall near her house and parked in front of an upscale department store noted for fine merchandise and excellent service.

Kate followed him docilely as he led the way to the costume-jewelry department without asking directions. The counters and glass display cases offered a bewildering variety of choices, but Garrett made his selection in a matter of minutes—a pair of gold hoop earrings.

"Aren't they kind of big?" Kate asked doubtfully, reaching for a pair of small bowknots.

"Don't even consider those." He clipped the hoops on her ears and surveyed the result approvingly. "We'll take these," he told the clerk, taking out his wallet and starting to hand her a credit card. Thinking better of it, he gave her cash instead.

"Let me pay for them." Kate opened her purse.

His hand closed over hers. "This is my gift to you."

"Why would you do that? We don't even know each other."

"Let's just say I want to."

She was flustered by the gesture and the husky tone of his voice. It would be nice to think Garrett was attracted to her, but that was extremely unlikely. He must be feeling sorry for her, which wasn't surprising after the way she'd bared her soul. Kate bitterly regretted those moments of self-indulgence.

"Perfect." He was gazing at her admiringly. "The finishing touch."

"Thank you," she mumbled, unable to look at him.

He squeezed her hand briefly. "Let's go get 'em, tiger."

The party was well under way when they arrived. A band was playing loudly, competing with the excited voices of the crowd. Couples were packed onto the dance floor, stopping every few feet to exchange greetings with long-lost friends. Other couples were sitting at tables or visiting back and forth between them. The large room was decorated in the school colors, with multicolored balloons and curls of paper streamers adding to the festive atmosphere.

Two women at a table near the entrance were chatting as they waited for latecomers. Kate recognized the slightly plump one as Sondra Purvis. She'd been on the fringes of the "in" group because of her willingness to do all the dreary jobs nobody else wanted to do. Like getting stuck at the door tonight checking names off a list while everyone else partied.

With barely a glance at Kate, she gave Garrett a big smile. "You must have been on the football team. How could I forget your name?"

"Possibly because you never knew it," Kate said crisply. "This is my guest. I'm Kate Beaumont."

Sondra looked at her blankly for a moment before pretending to recognize her. "Oh, sure. Glad you could come, Kate. I have your name tag right here. Sit anywhere you like. We didn't assign seating because we knew people would rather make up their own tables." She handed Kate an adhesive-backed white square with her name written in large black letters, then gave Garrett one marked Guest. "If you get bored when everybody starts reminiscing about the good old days, you can come back here and talk to me," she told him flirtatiously.

He smiled and took Kate's hand. "I could never get bored with Kate, but I appreciate your offer."

After they walked away, Kate withdrew her hand. This night was shaping up as the biggest mistake of her life. She felt more of an outsider than ever, and having Garrett see it for himself made the experience even worse.

"Shall we dance first and decide where to sit later?" he asked.

She nodded silently and let him lead her onto the floor.

Garrett did his best to fulfill his part of the bargain. He folded her in his arms and rested his cheek against her temple.

Kate held herself stiffly. "You don't have to put on an act. No one's watching."

He raised his head to look down at her. "I happen to be enjoying myself. I only wish you were."

"I let you down," she mumbled. "You were so sure your makeover was going to get results."

"For what it's worth, it got *my* attention." He smoothed the silky hair away from her face with subtly caressing fingers. "You're the loveliest woman here tonight."

"You haven't looked at the others."

"I don't want to." He held her close again, brushing his lips across her forehead.

Kate relaxed in his arms, feeling her spirits rise. Garrett must like her, to go to all this trouble. His standard services didn't require this kind of dedication. She rested her head on his shoulder, enjoying the solid feeling. Garrett's entire body gave her pleasure, as it had many women, without a doubt. What would it be like to have him make love to her? To feel his mouth burning a line of kisses across her skin? The very idea made her legs feel weak.

When the orchestra took a break, Kate said uncertainly, "I guess we should look for a table that has a couple of empty places."

"Let's be selective. We'll walk around and see what appeals to us."

Several people invited them to share their table, but Garrett made excuses. Kate didn't know why, but she did notice that he was garnering many second glances as they threaded their way through the throng. She didn't realize that much of the attention was directed at her.

Palmer Wesley was standing in the middle of a group, as he always had. Kate felt the years fall away as she looked at him and experienced a familiar tightness in her chest. He was even more handsome at twenty-eight than he'd been at eighteen. Men often improved with age, and Palmer was a classic example. His blond hair was still a crowning glory, although the boyish curls were tamed now by a trendy haircut. The superb physique was enhanced also by a well-tailored suit. Palmer had lived up to the yearbook's prediction. He looked successful, on top of the world, an unattainable as ever.

Kate was unaware of Garrett's comprehensive look at her rapt face, or the touch of amusement in his own expression as he read Palmer's name tag. She followed Garrett in a bemused state as he led her toward the group of people blocking the aisle.

Garrett stopped directly in front of Palmer. "Excuse us. Could we get by?"

"Sure." As Palmer started to move aside, his gaze passed over Kate and returned swiftly. He glanced at her name tag, then back to her face. "Well, hel—lo, Kate. Where have you been keeping yourself?"

"It's nice to see you again, Palmer," she said softly.

"It's been a long time." His eyes made a rapid circuit over her face and figure.

"Yes, it has."

"We have a lot of catching up to do. Tell me what's been happening to you." He flicked a glance at Garrett. "Are you married?"

"No. This is my guest." She introduced the two men.

"Why don't I leave you two to get reacquainted," Garrett suggested. "I'll go get us a drink."

"No!" Kate panicked at the thought of being left alone with Palmer. She was already having trouble thinking of things to say to him. "I'll go with you. We have to find a table."

"Sit here with us," Palmer invited.

"It looks full," Kate said doubtfully, gazing at the programs and evening purses cluttering almost every place.

"We can always add a couple more chairs."

"Good. Then we're all set. I'll be back in a few minutes." Garrett left before she could stop him.

Kate's palms were sweaty. How could she keep Palmer interested until Garrett returned? "Don't let me keep you from your . . . whoever you're with."

"I came alone so I could get around to seeing everybody without worrying about leaving my date sitting by herself in a corner."

"I thought surely you'd be married by this time."

"I'm glad I'm not, now." His voice deepened.

Having Palmer come on to her was a heady experience. "Everybody expected you and Betty Livingston to get married right after graduation."

"Good old Betty," he said fondly. "She'll be at our table tonight. I told her I'd save her a place."

"You still see her?"

"Once in a while. Betty married a doctor. They have a showplace in Beverly Hills—swimming pool, tennis court, the works. She's got it made in the shade."

"I'm not surprised. She was the prettiest girl in our class."

"I wouldn't say that." Palmer's attention returned to her. "I can't imagine why you and I never got together in high school."

"You were going steady with Betty."

"I'm not anymore," he murmured. "Can I phone you, Kate?"

She stared at him incredulously. It didn't seem possible that Palmer Wesley might actually ask her for a date.

When she didn't answer he said, "Do you have a permanent kind of thing going with that guy you're with?"

"Garrett? No, we . . . we're just friends."

"That's good news," Palmer said deeply.

Garrett returned with a drink in each hand. Since neither Kate nor Palmer noticed him, he was reluctant to announce his presence, correctly interpreting the scene. Before Garrett could move away, someone else broke up the intimate conversation.

Betty Livingston's arrival caused a flurry that no one could ignore. People rushed up to her calling excited greetings and exchanging social hugs and kisses. The man who trailed after her didn't seem to mind being overlooked. His admiration equaled that of her friends. Although she had a word for everyone, Betty's objective was Palmer.

He expressed delight at seeing her. "Where have you been? I was afraid you weren't going to show."

Her mouth thinned. "Kenny had one of his usual emergencies. I was about to come by myself."

Palmer glanced over Betty's shoulder at her husband. "Hi, Ken. Did one of your rich and famous patients have a tummy ache?"

"Something like that," he answered noncommittally.

"You'd have been in deep trouble if Betty missed the reunion."

"Don't I know it," Ken answered ruefully.

Betty dismissed any earlier unpleasantness. "Isn't this fun?" She glanced around, her lovely face lit with animation. "The whole class must be here tonight. Meg Appleton came down from Oregon, and I saw Tina Glaser. She has three children. Can you believe it?"

"Wait till you see Tony Serra's wife," Palmer advised. "You'll believe anything."

As they exchanged gossip, Garrett went over to Kate and handed her a drink. "Your high-school heartthrob certainly noticed you this time."

"Until Betty showed up," she answered wistfully. "She's even more gorgeous than she was in high school."

"Most people are. The common belief is that youth is wasted on the young, but I'll opt for maturity any day."

"Really? I'm surprised. You must have been a big man on campus. I'm sure your high-school years were more rewarding than your present—" She stopped in embarrassment.

Grinning wickedly, he said, "Don't be too sure. My present life is the fulfillment of a boyhood dream."

The lurid pictures that conjured up made her mouth thin disapprovingly. She kept forgetting the way Garrett made his living. A drumroll saved her from having to reply. They were asked to be seated so dinner could be served.

Chapter Two

The ballroom boiled with activity as everyone moved in a different direction. Kate hesitated as their table filled up, but Palmer hadn't forgotten her. He called for two more chairs and moved everyone over so Kate could sit next to him, with Garrett on the other side of her.

"You remember Kate Beaumont," Palmer said to Betty when they were all seated.

"Of course," she answered automatically, her eyes flicking to Garrett. "*We* haven't met, though," she said to him. "I'm Betty Buckston."

"And that's her husband, Ken," Palmer said.

When they had all acknowledged the introductions Betty said, "Where did you go to school, Garrett?"

"I graduated years ahead of you," he answered noncommittally.

"Not all that many," she protested.

"Betty likes older men," Palmer observed. "That's how Ken beat me out."

"I like to think it was more than age," Ken said mildly.

"Okay, you're richer than I am."

"You're terrible, Palmer." Betty's rebuke was perfunctory. "What business are you in, Garrett?"

"I suppose you could say public service." His blue eyes sparkled with merriment.

"I was told you're a doctor," Kate said hastily to Ken. "That must be a very fulfilling profession."

"The word is *rewarding*," Palmer corrected mockingly.

Their conversation was interrupted as the waiter placed salads in front of everyone and offered a choice of dressing.

During those few moments Kate remarked to Garrett in a low voice, "It didn't take Betty long to notice you."

"I'm sure she's only being polite," he answered.

"Not judging by Palmer's reaction. I think he's still in love with her."

"I doubt it. Your friend Palmer strikes me as the kind of man who wants to be the center of all female attention."

"You don't like him, do you?"

"I wouldn't say that," Garrett answered impassively. "I don't know him."

"He's really a wonderful person," Kate said eagerly. "Palmer was more than just a jock. He was also elected to the student council two years in a row. You'd really like him if you knew him."

"I'm sure you're right."

Kate wasn't fooled by Garrett's polite response. "I guess handsome men feel the same rivalry that beautiful women do."

"It's a compliment to be put in the same class as Palmer, knowing how you feel about him," Garrett commented ironically.

"I barely know the man," she protested. "I'll admit I had a crush on him in high school, but that was just kid stuff."

"You still think he's handsome, though," Garrett teased.

"I think *you're* handsome, too, but that doesn't mean I'm interested in you," she answered with annoyance.

"I'm crushed." His eyes twinkled. "I hoped this was the beginning of a beautiful friendship."

"I can't afford you," she said curtly.

"I give discounts to people I like," he murmured.

Before she could answer, Palmer joined their conversation. "You're not supposed to talk to each other at these things. You're supposed to reminisce about the happy times we shared."

"Garrett didn't go to Hollywood High," Kate reminded him.

"Where did you go?" Palmer asked Garrett the same questions Betty had asked earlier.

"I didn't go to school in Los Angeles," Garrett answered.

"You missed some rare old times. Didn't he, doll face?" Palmer put his arm around Kate and squeezed her shoulder.

"Yes," she agreed breathlessly.

Garrett's face was unreadable as he witnessed the gesture. "What do you do in the real world?" he asked the other man.

"I sell stocks and bonds." Palmer assessed Garrett's gold watch and expensive tie. "I have a couple of pretty hot offerings if you're interested."

"I'm not in the market right now, if you'll excuse the pun. But I'll keep you in mind," Garrett promised.

"I'll give you my card." Palmer removed his arm to reach into an inner pocket for a business card, which he handed to Garrett. "We can structure a complete portfolio for you."

"Can you believe how Palmer's changed?" Betty joined in from the other side of him. "He used to romance women. Now he's more interested in men."

"Only in a business sense," Palmer said. "A guy's got to make a living."

"Don't you find it a little tricky doing business with friends?" Garrett asked casually. "What happens when the stocks you recommended go down?"

"Hey, everything's a gamble. You don't get any guarantees in life."

"Palmer!" A man across the table leaned forward to get his attention. "What's your opinion of Sunrise Electronics? My broker warned me off it, but I read somewhere that they're developing some revolutionary new software."

"That's absolutely correct. Sunrise is high on our list of recommendations."

"Why do you think my broker turned thumbs down?"

"Let me tell you a few things about brokers." Palmer got up and went to pull a chair next to the other man. His face was completely absorbed.

Garrett watched with a mocking expression that he concealed when he turned to Kate. "Would you care to dance?"

Kate went into Garrett's arms a little diffidently, remembering her earlier encounter with his splendid physique. She would have left a discreet space between them, but he folded her close.

So close that she was aware of his hard chest against her yielding breasts, and the breadth of his shoulders under her hand. She held herself rigidly as their thighs brushed, hoping he didn't feel the tiny quiver that ran through her.

"Are you having a good time?" he asked.

His slightly husky voice was another disturbance. When he spoke softly in her ear like that, a simple question sounded seductive. The man was unbelievably sexy. Women a lot more experienced than she would react to him, Kate assured herself.

"I'm having a wonderful time," she answered. "I can't believe I've actually been accepted by all the people who barely knew I was alive."

"Do you find them changed?"

"Not at all! That's what's so wonderful. They're even more glamorous."

"They're the kind of people you'd like to associate with regularly?"

"I'm sorry if you're not enjoying yourself," she said coolly.

"I'm having a very interesting evening, and I wasn't being critical. It was an innocent question."

"It didn't sound that way," she said resentfully. "Someone like you can't understand what it's like to be an outsider. I know tonight won't change my life, but this one evening makes up for a lot. I don't feel like an ugly duckling anymore."

"Then perhaps this night *will* change your life."

"No. Tomorrow we'll all go back to our own worlds and nothing will be any different."

"You never can tell," he replied softly.

The music stopped and they returned to the table to find the entrees were being served. Conversation was general for a while, as they all ate dinner.

When the orchestra resumed playing, Palmer asked Kate to dance. She followed him onto the floor feeling seventeen years old again. Her mouth was dry as she moved awkwardly into his arms, all her natural grace deserting her.

Kate dimly registered the fact that Palmer wasn't as tall as Garrett, nor did his body have the same tensile strength. If she hadn't been so dazzled, she would have realized Palmer's well-tailored suit was partly responsible for the width of his shoulders. But he still radiated the same charm and confidence that had beguiled her as a teenager.

"I've been wanting to get you in my arms all night," he said softly in her ear.

Kate was infatuated, but she wasn't stupid. "Me and the rest of the student body," she commented dryly.

"Only the girls." He laughed. "And out of those, only the attractive ones."

"Well, at least you're honest."

"I'll be anything you want me to be," he murmured.

As she started to melt, a voice said, "Palmer, old buddy!" The male half of a couple dancing next to them punched Palmer playfully on the shoulder. "How you doin'?"

"Couldn't be better," Palmer answered jovially. "It's been a while. What's new in your life, Slim Jim?"

"You're looking at her." Jim introduced his wife.

After introductions were made all around, the other couple moved away and Palmer said, "Where were we?"

"I don't remember," Kate lied. "Tell me about yourself, Palmer. Why did you and Betty break up after going together for so long?"

He shrugged. "I wasn't ready to settle down and she was."

"Ken seems like a nice man," Kate said tentatively.

"He's perfect for her," Palmer answered with a cynical expression. "A rich workaholic who gives her lots of freedom."

Kate glanced over at their table. Betty had moved to the vacant place beside Garrett and was talking to him animatedly.

After following her gaze, Palmer laughed shortly. "Don't worry about your boyfriend. Betty doesn't play for keeps. She's not about to throw away a good thing."

"Are you saying she married Ken for his money?"

Palmer's mouth curved as he looked at her startled face. "Sweet, naive little Kate. You're adorable."

"I'm serious, Palmer. That's a terrible thing to say."

"On the contrary. It's one of the more sensible reasons for getting married. Love doesn't necessarily last, but money is something you can always count on."

"If that's the way you feel, it's a good thing you never married."

"Actually, I was married briefly. It didn't work out." His handsome face wore a sardonic look. "That's how I got to be an authority on the subject."

Kate understood his cynicism now. It covered a deep hurt. "I'm sorry," she said in a muted voice.

"Don't be." He drew her closer. "If I were tied down I'd miss this opportunity with you."

Someone else interrupted them with an enthusiastic greeting. "I've been looking all over for you, Palmer, old pal. You've been one step ahead of me all night."

"Just like the old days." Palmer laughed. "What have you been doing with yourself all these years, Mugsy?"

"I'm in the construction game. How about you? I kept expecting to see your name in the paper. I thought for sure you'd turn out to be the star quarterback for the Rams."

"He could never top the pass that won the game for us against L.A. High," the man's partner joined in.

They formed a little oasis in the middle of the dance floor while the two men and the other woman recalled the past. Kate didn't join in.

When they finally moved away, Palmer said nostalgically, "It's great to see the old crowd again, isn't it?"

"It must be nice to be as popular as you are," she answered evasively.

"Don't tell me you don't know."

"I wasn't a big football star."

"You have other talents," he murmured, moving his hand slowly down her back.

"Actually I do," she said, wanting to impress him with her accomplishments.

Palmer didn't give her a chance. "We'll have to discuss them one night soon." He looked over her shoulder. "Here comes one of the Henderson twins. They were real characters. Remember them?"

"I guess so," Kate said hopelessly. Every time Palmer started to make a date, they were interrupted.

Garrett's eyes strayed to Kate often as she circled the floor with Palmer. The rest of the time he listened to Betty with a faint smile on his face, parrying her questions adroitly.

"This must be terribly dull for you," she commented. "I know Kenny loathes these things."

"Why don't we ask him to join us?" Garrett glanced over at the other man, who was pretending to be interested in what the woman next to him was saying.

"Laura's trying to get free medical advice about her baby's rash." Betty laughed merrily. "She doesn't realize Ken is a surgeon."

"Shouldn't we rescue the poor man?"

"He can take care of himself." Betty shrugged. "You never did tell me what you do."

"Does it matter?"

Her eyes went over him appreciatively. "Not really. I like mysterious men."

"That could be dangerous," he answered lightly.

"A little danger adds spice to life."

Garrett assessed her high-fashion gown and expensive jewelry. "I wouldn't imagine anything was missing from your life."

"Appearances can be deceiving," she murmured.

He grinned suddenly. "How very true."

"You're so easy to talk to. Why don't you come over some afternoon for a swim in the pool?" she asked artlessly. "We could get to know each other better."

"I'd like that." Garrett glanced over at Ken and said swiftly. "Your husband's eyes are glazing over. We have to give him emergency relief. Ken, could you join us and settle an argument?" he called to the other man.

"I'm in your debt for life," Ken declared when he'd moved to the empty chair next to them. "What would you like? A free gall-bladder operation? An appendectomy?"

Garrett smiled. "I'd prefer to keep all my spare parts if you don't mind."

"Now I know why I decided to be a surgeon," Ken said. "A patient can't talk when she has a mask over her nose and mouth."

"You're a medical man. You're supposed to listen to people's symptoms," Betty told him.

"How do I know what to do if Johnny won't eat his strained peas?"

Garrett chuckled. "You can suggest she give him an aperitif. That's supposed to improve the appetite."

Betty was bored with the conversation. "We're sitting here like a bunch of chaperons. Dance with me, Garrett."

"It would be a pleasure, but your husband has priority."

"Ken hates to dance." Betty pushed her chair back.

"Go ahead," Ken said agreeably. "I've been on my feet all day."

"You have a very understanding husband," Garrett remarked when he and Betty were on the dance floor.

"Yes, Ken is a darling." She looked with more immediate interest at Garrett. "How did a handsome hunk like you escape marriage all these years?"

"It wasn't deliberate. Like Palmer, I'm still looking."

"For a rich woman?" she asked derisively.

"Is that his goal?"

"I shouldn't have said that. Palmer is really a fun guy. We went together for a long time."

"So Kate told me."

Betty gazed at him speculatively. "How well do you know her?"

He smiled winningly. "Can a man ever say he really knows a beautiful woman?"

She frowned slightly. "Do you have some deep, dark secret you're trying to hide? I can't get you to answer a single question."

"You said you like mysterious men."

"Up to a point. You've piqued my curiosity now. I intend to find out everything about you," she warned.

"That could be a mistake. I might turn out to be very disappointing."

"I doubt that. However, I will admit it might take longer than just this one evening to figure you out."

His expression was amused. "That presents a problem, since tonight is all we have."

"Not necessarily. I've decided to have a party next Saturday night and you're invited. I'll take a refusal personally," she added.

His amusement turned to thoughtfulness. "Is Kate included in the invitation?"

"If you'd like," Betty answered tepidly.

After a moment's hesitation Garrett said, "We accept with pleasure."

When everyone was seated at the table once more, Betty clapped her hands for attention. "Listen up everybody. Ken and I are having a post-reunion party next Saturday night and you're all invited."

Everybody but Kate greeted the idea with enthusiasm. As she opened her mouth to decline, Garrett made that awkward.

"I've already accepted for both of us," he said.

"How could you do a thing like that?" she asked in a furious whisper.

"I thought you'd be pleased."

"Are you out of your mind? Now I'll have to hire you again."

Before he could answer, Betty put her hand on his arm. "What do you think about making it a pool party?"

"That sounds nice," he agreed absently.

When Garrett turned back to Kate, her eyes were sparkling angrily. "I'm beginning to get the picture. You accepted because you want to see Betty again. Don't you have any scruples?"

"You told me these were the people you always wanted to be friendly with," he answered patiently. "I thought this would give you the opportunity."

"The fact that your own interests were being served had nothing to do with it, I suppose."

"I won't charge for my time." He smiled.

"You must be very attracted to Betty," Kate said scathingly.

"As a matter of fact, she isn't my type. Whether you believe it or not, I was doing this for you. If you don't want to go, that's fine with me. We'll make our excuses."

Kate was torn in two directions. She'd get to see Palmer again, and maybe at a smaller party he'd finally ask for a date. It was also a chance to be accepted into their select group after all these years. The drawback was Garrett. If anyone ever discovered their arrangement, she'd die of shame. But he'd carried it off well tonight. One more time should be safe.

"What's your decision?" he asked.

Her eyes were on Palmer's classic profile. "Well, since you've already accepted . . ."

"I thought you'd see it that way," he said dryly.

The evening flew by for Kate, and she assumed it did for Garrett, also. He got along well with the men, and she noticed that the women flirted with him openly. But most of her attention was centered on Palmer. Kate wasn't aware of the indulgent way Garrett's eyes followed her, or the occasional surreptitious glance he took at his watch.

When the reunion was over and they were driving home he asked, "Was it everything you expected?"

"More than I could have hoped for, thanks to you," she answered happily. "I'm sorry I was so mean about Betty. Naturally you were attracted to her. What man wouldn't be?"

"It's time you grew up, Kate," Garrett said impatiently. "You're not a plain-Jane anymore, and she's not head cheerleader."

Kate fingered the gold hoops in her ears. "It takes more than a short skirt and a pair of earrings to make you feel different inside."

"That will happen sooner than you think." His voice was gentler.

"Palmer did seem interested," she said eagerly. "Do you think he'll call me?"

"I hope so." Garrett's jaw squared. "You won't get him out of your system any other way."

"I can't understand this unreasonable dislike you have for Palmer."

"You can do better."

"You're talking to a woman who had to hire herself a date," she reminded him wryly.

"It happened to work out this time, but you're not to do that again," he said a trifle grimly.

"If you were serious about offering your services free, I can't accept," she replied. "This is your livelihood. I intend to pay for your time next week."

He pulled up in front of her apartment house and turned off the motor. "Let's go inside, Kate. We have to talk." He got out of the car before she could stop him.

Kate turned on the lights in the living room, feeling slightly awkward with Garrett suddenly. Surely he didn't think she expected any more from the evening?

"Would you, uh, like some coffee?" she asked. "I'm afraid I don't have anything stronger."

"Nothing, thanks. Sit down, Kate, I have a confession to make."

"You don't have to tell me anything," she said swiftly.

During the long evening, Kate had managed to forget the way Garrett made his living, and she didn't want to be reminded now. He'd been so supportive that she'd started to think of him as a friend, someone she could even be attracted to under different circumstances. There was a definite chemistry present when they danced together.

"Unfortunately I do." He sighed. "I meant well, but things kind of got out of hand."

"I thought everything went off very well," she said uncertainly.

"I'm pleased for your sake, but I have to set the record straight between us. I'm not what you think I am."

"I shouldn't have been so judgmental," she said repentantly. "You have a right to live your life any way you like."

"Everyone does. But I don't make my living from women." He gave a small laugh. "Well, not exactly."

Kate didn't want to hear any of the lurid details. She stood up hastily. "I really feel like some coffee. Are you sure you won't have a cup?"

"Will you listen to me, Kate?" Garrett's hands on her shoulders forced her to face him. "I'm not a paid escort. I'm the president and CEO of the Carriage House department-store chain."

She stared at him blankly for a moment. "You don't really expect me to believe that?"

"I can understand why you wouldn't, but it's true."

"I'm flattered that you care what I think, but couldn't you have made up a more believable story?" she teased gently.

"Didn't you wonder why I wouldn't talk about myself? Not even about where I went to school?"

"You didn't want anyone to guess why you were there. Where *did* you go to school?" She'd wondered about that at the time.

"I attended a well-known prep school back east. But if I'd mentioned the name you'd either have thought I was lying or you would have started to wonder why I settled for being a professional escort."

Kate was thoroughly confused. "I can't say I approve, but I can guess why. That man at the agency said you were one of his highest-paid employees."

"That was his little joke. Foster Gray and I have known each other all our lives. His mother and mine serve on charity boards together."

She was still struggling to understand. "Is that really his business?"

"His latest one. Foster is one of those people who are always looking for a way to make a fast buck. Some of the things he comes up with are slightly shabby. That's what I was doing there that day, trying to get him to give up this latest nonsense."

Could Garrett possibly be telling the truth? Little things started to click into place. Foster's incredulity when Garrett volunteered for her job, the way Garrett knew exactly where the jewelry department was when they stopped to buy the earrings at the Carriage House, why he put away the credit card with his name on it and gave the salesclerk cash instead.

As everything became blindingly clear, Kate's temper erupted. "You couldn't resist joining him in a small practical joke, could you? What a laugh that's going to get when you tell the story to all your socially correct friends. The mighty Garrett Richmond taking a drab little mouse to her public-school reunion and getting *paid* for it."

"You're being unfair, Kate." He didn't know which accusation to refute first. "I have no intention of telling anyone about tonight, and you'll get your money back."

"No thanks! I'm going to frame that canceled check as a reminder not to trust another man as long as I live!"

"I don't know why you're so angry. I'll admit I wasn't completely candid with you, but I fulfilled my part of the bargain. Why does it matter that I'm not what you thought I was?"

"You were making fun of me," she said bitterly. "I made an honest mistake when I thought you were one of the escorts. Why didn't you set me straight?"

"That would have embarrassed you horribly, and you were already insecure about what you were doing."

"You could have said you were already booked for tonight. You didn't have to go through this elaborate charade."

"I could tell this evening meant a great deal to you. I didn't want you to be disappointed," he said quietly.

Her slender body stiffened. "I don't appreciate your pity."

He folded his arms and stared at her consideringly. "Actually I do feel sorry for you. You're the most mixed-up woman I've ever encountered."

"I can just imagine the kind of airheads you run around with," she flared. "I may not be able to match their bra size, but I hold a very responsible position. My work makes a contribution to society."

"Do you enjoy it?"

"Of course I do! It's fascinating."

"They why didn't you mention it even once tonight?"

"Well, they...nobody was interested."

"That's not the reason, Kate. You were so dazzled by your high-school idols that it never occurred to you that you've come a lot farther than they have."

"How can you say that? Didn't you see how everyone flocked around them?"

"Is that your goal in life? To be popular?"

"Not solely, but it would be nice. You make popularity sound like something to be ashamed of," she protested.

"I suppose you'd think it was flattery if I said you have more to offer than Palmer and Betty."

"We'd both know you were merely trying to build my self-esteem."

"That's exactly what I intend to do. You want to be a member of their inner circle? Okay, I'll help you. But I'm betting that within a month your priorities are going to change."

"If you fancy yourself as some latter day Pygmalion, forget it. I realize now that you're the reason I was invited to Betty's party."

"You didn't give her much reason to find you interesting," he said calmly.

Kate gave him an indignant glare. "Women like Betty are only interested in men."

"Now you're learning," Garrett said with satisfaction. "You could never be like her except on the surface, so that's what we'll have to work on."

"You're going to make me look like Betty?" Kate asked incredulously.

"In a manner of speaking. Come to my store Monday morning and we'll begin your metamorphosis."

"Do you really think a new dress is going to make a difference?"

"It's a start. Stop in my office when you get there."

"Even if I put any stock in your theory, I have to work on Monday."

"Can't you take a day off?"

"I suppose so." She had a lot of vacation time coming. "But I'd have to tell them ahead of time. I can't simply fail to show up."

"I wish all *my* people were as dependable," he said wryly. "All right, make it Tuesday, then. If you get through in time, I'll take you to lunch."

"How long can it take to buy a dress?" she asked, wondering why she was agreeing in the first place.

"I have more that that planned for you. Put yourself in my hands and prepare to have your life changed."

"Why do you care what I do with my life?" she asked slowly.

Garrett had asked himself the same question many times during the previous week. The answer wasn't clear. All he got was a picture of a vulnerable young woman badly in need of a friend.

"Why are you bothering with me?" she persisted.

"Maybe I'm tired of airheads." He looked her up and down mischievously. "And just for the record, there's nothing wrong with your bra size." As color swiftly raced to her cheeks he framed her face in his palms, becoming serious. "I enjoyed tonight. I hope you did, too."

Before she could move away, he kissed her. It was a brief kiss, certainly not passionate, but Kate's body tingled in unaccustomed places. She had an insane desire to fling her arms around his neck and press closely against him. Luckily total shock froze her in place.

The spell was broken when he left. With the return of common sense, Kate began to question Garrett's motives. He must be a very sought-after bachelor. Maybe he'd chalked tonight up to a good deed, but why was he willing to waste another Saturday night? The answer to that wasn't hard to figure out. Betty had made another conquest.

As Kate got undressed she felt an unreasoning resentment. Garrett certainly didn't mean anything to her, but she was disappointed in his lack of principles. He could get all the women he wanted, without having to stoop to a flirtation with a married woman. Kate also objected to being used as a smoke screen to cover their sophisticated little dalliance.

If it weren't for Palmer, she wouldn't even bother going to the party next week. Betty had proved to be something of a disappointment. She was even more beautiful, but she'd changed since high school.

Palmer hadn't, though. He was still as handsome and charming as she remembered. And maybe even within reach this time around! Kate closed her eyes blissfully. But as she drifted off to sleep an unaccountable thing happened. She dreamed of lips that moved sensuously over hers. And they were Garrett's.

Kate had always looked forward to going to work on Monday, especially since her weekends were usually uneventful. But that Monday her mind was on other things. The reunion had made her realize there was more to life than work, no matter how fulfilling it was.

On the way to the director's office to ask for Tuesday off, Kate made a lightning decision. Why not request the whole week off? She hadn't taken any of her vacation time, and the year was half over already.

The director seemed startled by the request. "Is there an emergency in your family, Miss Beaumont?"

"No, I just have some things I want to do," she answered.

He looked at her disapprovingly. "Well, I don't know. Eric's been out with another bad cold, and Dwight's wife is pregnant. He's missed a lot of work. We're really behind schedule right now."

Kate knew that Eric's "bad colds" were more often hangovers, and Dwight had already made his contribution toward his wife's pregnancy. Both men had also taken their vacations.

"I've never asked for time off before," she reminded the director.

"And we appreciate your dedication," he assured her smoothly. "It's just that this is a bad time. Maybe next month. I'll see what I can do."

Kate suddenly rebelled against all the patronizing she'd taken. She wasn't just a warm body on the payroll. If she weren't a competent scientist, they would have fired her long ago.

"I'll go ahead with plans for next month, then," she said firmly. "But I still need tomorrow off."

He looked at her calm, adamant face. "I'm sure that won't be any problem. Just mention it to your supervisor."

Kate was checking slides under a microscope that afternoon when her coworker Dwight stood up and started unbuttoning his white lab coat.

Placing a sheaf of papers next to her, he said, "Check these figures for me, will you? I have to cut out."

A glance at the wall clock told her it was three-thirty. "Sorry, but I have to finish this experiment today."

"You can do mine afterward. It will only take ten or fifteen minutes."

"Then why can't you do it?" she asked.

"Amy's mother is expecting us for dinner, and they live way up in the boondocks. I want to beat the traffic on the freeway."

"I'd like to get home at a reasonable hour, too."

"Come on! You live right here in the city."

"Did it ever occur to you that I might have something to do after work, also?"

He gave her a startled look, as though it were a new idea. "You never minded before."

"I met someone this weekend who gave me a whole new slant on life," she answered ironically.

"That's great," Dwight said uncertainly. "I guess I never thought about you having a personal life."

"I guess I never did, either," Kate replied.

Her emancipator was having his own problems. The conversation with the woman he'd been dating frequently wasn't going well.

"I can't believe you're breaking another date!" Lorna Jameson's voice vibrated with anger.

"We didn't really have a date," Garrett protested.

"When you canceled last Saturday you told me you'd see me next weekend."

"How about Sunday night? That's still the weekend."

"The country-club dance is *Saturday* night," she said irately.

"They have them regularly."

"Are you trying to tell me something, Garrett? I don't appreciate being kept dangling. If you're dumping me, at least have the decency to say so."

He smothered a sigh. "You date other men, Lorna. It isn't as though we've made any commitment to each other."

"I'd be willing to. You're the one who doesn't want to get involved."

"I've been concerned about that lately. I don't think I'm being fair to you, Lorna."

"Don't say that." She dropped her complaints abruptly. "I didn't mean to be unreasonable. If you can't make it Saturday night, you can't make it. I understand."

"I'm really sorry."

"Don't worry about it. Freddy Clayborne asked me to go with him. I'll simply call him back."

"At least I'm glad I didn't spoil your weekend."

"I didn't say that," she answered softly. "I'd rather be with you."

"That's sweet," he replied automatically.

"I'll see you on Sunday, then."

"I'm looking forward to it." His expression wasn't as eager as his words. Garrett's face cleared when his secretary came in to deliver a message.

"I made all the arrangements for Miss Beaumont tomorrow, as you instructed."

"Good. Keep all my appointments flexible."

Chapter Three

Garrett ran the far-flung Carriage House chain from a large corner suite of offices on the top floor of the main store. A visitor had to pass by a receptionist and his private secretary, Sylvia Taylor, before getting in to see him.

Kate got only as far as the secretary's office on that Tuesday morning. The woman was expecting her, however. She made a brief call on a house telephone, then gave Kate her full attention.

"Mr. Richmond is in a meeting right now, but he made all the arrangements. I've assigned Rosemary to assist you. I'm sure you'll find her very helpful." Sylvia's professionally gracious manner didn't betray the hint of curiosity in her eyes.

Kate was annoyed. Did Garrett think her taste was that bad? "I don't need anyone to help me select a dress," she said coolly.

"The choice will be yours, naturally," Sylvia answered smoothly. "Rosemary will merely show you our newest arrivals. Personal shoppers can help you assemble a wardrobe in half the time."

"What is a personal shopper?" Kate asked warily.

"She'll bring accessories to you while you're trying on gowns, everything you need to complete the outfit. So much easier than having to visit all the various departments yourself."

The difference between a gown and a dress could run into a lot of money. Kate began having serious second thoughts. The reference to a wardrobe and accessories bothered her, also. What had she gotten herself into?

"I think I'd better speak to Mr. Richmond," she said firmly.

"I'm afraid he'll be tied up for quite a while, but he definitely wants to see you after you're finished." Before Kate could insist, Sylvia consulted a slip of paper on her desk. "Your appointment with Philippe is at eleven-thirty."

"Who is Philippe?" Kate asked blankly.

"Our top hairstylist. I think you'll be pleased with his work."

"I don't want my hair styled." Kate was beginning to feel like Alice in Wonderland talking to the Red Queen. This conversation wasn't making any more sense.

"It's complimentary," Sylvia said gently.

"That isn't why...I don't want Garrett to..."

As Kate paused to take a deep breath, a very chic young woman entered the office. Her hair and makeup were works of art, and her black dress showed off a model's figure.

Giving Kate a smile that displayed even white teeth, she said, "This is a real pleasure, Miss Beaumont. I'm Rosemary."

"I know you're anxious to get started," Sylvia said. "I'll see you later, Miss Beaumont."

Kate found herself walking down the hall to the elevator alongside Rosemary, without quite knowing how she'd let this happen.

"You're really in luck," the other woman remarked. "We've just received a shipment of truly stunning things. The casual wear is classic, and the evening clothes are absolutely divine."

Kate struggled to regain control. "There's been some kind of misunderstanding. I came in to buy one dress, and I don't even need that actually. The party I'm invited to turned into a pool party."

"You'll want to see some bikinis, then. We have a darling pink one with a matching cover-up."

Kate decided they must speak a different language in this store. "I don't wear bikinis," she said wearily.

"Why not? You have the perfect figure for it." She scanned Kate's body knowledgeably. "You're a size six, aren't you?"

"Yes, but I wouldn't be comfortable in anything that skimpy."

Rosemary laughed. "Better you than the size sixteens who wear them."

They'd reached a room with beige couches and glass cocktail tables. No racks of clothes were in sight, and there were no other customers.

While Rosemary was seating Kate and offering coffee, a saleswoman approached. She was introduced as Clarice.

"Show Miss Beaumont the Federico Gilly suits first," Rosemary instructed. "They're quite outstanding this year."

Kate had always considered a suit something service-able to wear to work or a business meeting. She changed her mind when she saw the outfits Clarice brought for her inspection. These weren't plain skirts and jackets. The fabrics were rich and softly draped, and they were imaginatively designed to be simple, yet not severe. Although Kate was afraid they were much too expensive, she couldn't resist choosing several to try on.

But when she would have followed Clarice to the dressing room, Rosemary said, "Why don't you make your other selections first, then we'll take everything in at once for you."

"I don't need anything else," Kate objected.

"You might change your mind when you see the rest of the collection."

As Kate was about to put her foot down, Clarice returned carrying an armload of shimmering garments in rainbow hues. She held up an evening gown that effectively silenced Kate's protest. One long paisley chiffon skirt was slit almost to mid-thigh. The skirt was topped by a short jacket completely covered with bronze sequins in a paisley pattern. It was a gown that promised dreams would come true. Kate's eyes kept straying back to it while Clarice brought out everything from pants to afternoon dresses.

Finally Rosemary glanced at her watch and said, "Perhaps you'd better start trying on some of these things. You don't want to be late for your appointment with Philippe. Clarice will assist you, while I go and gather up a few accessories."

Kate started with the suits, which were all wildly flattering. They had short skirts that showed off her long, slim legs, and they fit perfectly. When Rosemary returned with a wide leather belt and a brightly patterned scarf, Kate looked as though she'd stepped out of the pages of a fashion magazine.

"The right accessories really make an outfit, don't they?" Rosemary was gazing at her admiringly. "I brought these gold chains to go with the taupe-and-white check. That's going to look elegant on you."

"How much is it?" Kate asked doubtfully. "I can't seem to find any price tags."

"Mr. Richmond said he'd discuss that with you."

"What is there to discuss? All I want to know is the price."

"I'm not exactly sure. Perhaps he intends to give you a discount as a special customer," Rosemary said delicately.

Color flooded Kate's clear skin as she caught the implication. "Mr. Richmond has no reason to do me a favor. We don't even know each other very well."

"He wants all our customers to be satisfied," Rosemary answered urbanely.

They both knew not everyone got this much personalized attention. But Kate realized any further disclaimers on her part would only confirm the woman's suspicions. Did Garrett have any idea what he'd done?

Since she didn't want to put up any more fuss, Kate tried on one outfit after another, even the pink bikini Rosemary had brought from the sportswear department. The two women assured her that it was sensational on her, and Kate had to admit she looked sexy. Would she really have the nerve to wear it at Betty's next Saturday? One thing was certain. If Palmer didn't ask her for a date when he saw her wearing this, then she might as well put the dream to sleep for good.

"I don't like to rush you, but Philippe can get quite temperamental when he's kept waiting," Rosemary prodded gently as Kate stared dreamily into the mirror.

"I'll have these things sent out today," Clarice promised.

Kate snapped out of her reverie. "No, don't do that. Put them on hold until I speak with Mr. Richmond."

Rosemary walked her to the beauty salon and turned Kate over to the receptionist, who took her to a dressing room and gave her a powder-blue smock to change into.

Kate hadn't intended to keep the appointment, but her hair needed a trim, and this was a perfect opportunity since she had the day off. Usually she was forced to sandwich a trip to the beauty salon between all the other Saturday errands. Her annoyance at Garrett's high-handedness faded slightly as she hung up her brown jacket and unbuttoned her beige cotton blouse.

When she was seated in a chair, Philippe combed his fingers through her hair, spreading it out wide. "You have glorious hair," he proclaimed. "Why haven't you done anything with it?"

"Like what?" she asked.

"Cutting! Styling! Color!"

"I don't want my hair color changed," she said in alarm.

"Not changed—enhanced."

"All I want is a little trim," she answered adamantly.

He tilted the chair back and started to shampoo her hair. "If you want a trim you go to a barber. I'm going to give you a whole new image."

"I don't know what you've been told, but I'm perfectly happy with myself the way I am."

"You must let your imagination soar. A new hairdo does more for a woman than a new lover. You don't wear last year's dresses, do you? Why settle for last year's hairstyle?"

Kate could have told him her wardrobe was much older than that, but he probably wouldn't have listened. Nobody did. Phillippe's eyes were narrowed as he picked up a pair of scissors and lifted strands of hair at random.

Since it was too late to do anything about it, Kate crossed her fingers and hoped for the best as tiny bits of hair floated to the floor.

Philippe worked swiftly and silently. Finally he laid down the scissors and called to an assistant, "Mix me three parts of Golden Sunlight and one part Autumn Haze."

"I told you I didn't want my hair dyed," Kate said apprehensively.

"Hair that looks dyed is an abomination," he agreed absently, ruffling the damp tendrils with his fingers until the assistant brought him a small bowl. Tilting Kate back once more, he poured a pungent smelling liquid through her hair.

"What's that stuff?" she exclaimed.

"Marsha will wash you out in ten minutes," he said without answering her question. "Call her if you're uncomfortable."

Kate was immobilized with her head in the sink. Murderous thoughts crossed her mind, but she was unable to act on them.

"Would you like some lunch, Miss Beaumont?" a perky voice asked.

"You have no idea what I'd like," Kate grated.

"We have a very nice chicken salad," the unseen woman informed her. "Or perhaps you'd like a cup of soup and some tea sandwiches."

"What kind of dye did Philippe put on my hair?" Kate demanded.

"It's not a dye, just a rinse."

"You mean it will wash out?"

"In time," was the unreassuring response. "Have you decided on your lunch order?"

Kate threw in the towel. She'd wandered into an alien world, and starving herself wouldn't do any good. Besides, she had a feeling she was going to need all her strength. With a sigh of resignation Kate ordered a chicken salad and iced tea.

During the next several hours she received every kind of service imaginable. After her hair was shampooed again, Philippe wound it on large pink rollers. While he was working on her, a manicurist rolled over a table containing a bewildering array of bottles and jars.

"Would you like a French manicure?" she asked.

Kate shrugged. "Why not?" She didn't even know what a French manicure was, but it would probably go with Philippe's hairdo. No sense in doing things halfway.

When she emerged from under the hair dryer, another young woman seated her at a long counter. Kate thought she was going to remove the rollers, but instead she poured lotion on a cotton pad and started to dab at Kate's face.

"What are you doing?" Kate exclaimed.

"I'm here to do your makeup, Miss Beaumont. My name is Caroline."

After cleansing her skin, Caroline applied cosmetics like an artist creating a living masterpiece. Two shades of eye shadow brought out the green and gold of Kate's hazel eyes, then mascara darkened her long, silky lashes. A whisper of blush highlighted her cheekbones after they were dusted with translucent powder.

"What are you wearing tonight?" Caroline asked.

"Does it matter?" Kate asked with a puzzled look.

"I want to know what color lipstick to use."

Kate didn't know how to tell her she'd probably be watching television in her bathrobe. Before she had to confess the shameful truth, Philippe appeared to comb her out.

He turned her away from the mirror while he brushed and combed, keeping up a running commentary. "Ah, yes. See the way it's layered for fullness? Look at the shape. Isn't it exquisite?"

"She looks fabulous," Caroline agreed dutifully.

"Can I see?" Kate asked with some apprehension.

"In a minute." Philippe fussed for a little longer, then twirled the chair around with a flourish. "Well, what do you say now?"

Kate couldn't say anything. A stranger looked back at her from the mirror. This woman had a tumble of shining, sun-tipped hair framing a delicately tinted face. She looked serenely in command of herself and everyone around her.

"You really are a genius," Kate whispered.

"Of course." Philippe took a final look and walked away.

"He might have admitted he had a lot to work with," Caroline said disgustedly, but she was careful to keep her voice low. "Have you decided what color lipstick you'd like?"

Kate glanced back at her image. How could she waste all this artistry in front of the TV? She could hardly bear to get back into her plain suit and tailored blouse. Suddenly rebellion took over.

"I have some things on hold in the gown shop. One of them is a purple wool dress. Could somebody bring it to me?"

"Certainly, Miss Beaumont. And I have the perfect lipstick to go with it—Rosy Wine."

The dress arrived accompanied by high-heeled gunmetal-gray pumps and a matching quilted purse. Rosemary's taste was once again unerring. They were the perfect daytime accessories for the slim, jewel-toned dress. It didn't matter that Kate had nowhere to go. Just feeling this confident was a heady experience.

She only regretted that her metamorphosis had taken so long. Lunch in a fancy restaurant with Garrett would have been the perfect climax to this surreal day. He was probably tied up by now. But maybe not.

As she hesitated about stopping by his office, Kate remembered she had to settle the matter of money. She didn't know the cost of the things she'd tentatively selected, or even the outfit she had on.

Her fears about disturbing Garrett were groundless. "He's been waiting for you, Miss Beaumont," Sylvia informed her.

Garrett was talking on the phone when Kate was shown in. He glanced up absently to say, "I'll be with you in a minute." As he got a good look at her, his eyes widened. "I'll have to call you back, Doug," he told the caller.

Garrett came around from behind the desk, inspecting Kate from her shining crown to her stylish pumps. "You look fantastic!"

"I should. It took long enough. I'm sorry about lunch. Can I have a rain check?" Kate was surprised at her own request. She'd never asked a man that before.

"Any time!" he answered enthusiastically. "But how about cocktails right now?"

"That would be lovely." Her face lit up.

"I just have to sign a few letters and then we can go. Make yourself comfortable on the couch. Unless you'd like to do some more shopping."

"No, I've done more than enough," she answered ruefully. "I have to talk to you about that."

"Was everyone helpful?"

"They were wonderful, except for one thing. Nobody would tell me the price of anything."

"Don't worry about it."

"I'm not worried, I simply want to know. I picked out a lot of things, and I have to know if I should take all of them."

"Let's call them my gift to you."

"I'm not a charity case," she replied distantly. "I make an excellent salary, and I can afford to pay for my own clothes."

"I didn't mean to be patronizing," he said mildly. "All right, I'll give them to you at cost."

"That's not acceptable, either. You don't give discounts to your other customers. Why should you do it for me?"

"Anyone who has to make money from his friends should get into another line of work."

"We've known each other less than a week," she pointed out.

"Time is no measure of friendship." He smiled, rummaging through some papers on his desk. "They sent up a memo on your purchases." After doing some mental arithmetic, he mentioned an amount that made her gasp.

"They came to that much?"

Garrett hid a look of amusement. "That's for a whole wardrobe."

"True. I haven't been shopping in so long, I guess I forgot about inflation."

"Did you enjoy yourself?"

"Tremendously! I may have found a new hobby." She laughed.

"You're welcome any time," he said, scribbling his name rapidly at the bottom of several letters.

Garrett took her to the cocktail lounge of a well-known restaurant on Sunset Boulevard. Although it was too early for the dining room to open, the bar was fairly crowded.

When they were seated on a leather banquette and had ordered drinks, Garrett gave Kate his full attention. His gaze roved approvingly over the blouson top of the purple dress. "Is that part of your new wardrobe? You have excellent taste."

"Rosemary does, anyway," Kate answered with a small laugh.

"Why do you always put yourself down?"

"I don't in my own field," she said defensively. "But the world of high fashion is new to me."

"You'll get used to it rapidly. My grandfather built an empire on the desire women have to be attractive. And he never even heard the slogan—When the going gets tough, the tough go shopping." Garrett laughed.

Kate's face was troubled. "There's something wrong with depending on clothes to give you confidence."

"Everyone has some kind of talisman. Have you ever watched a big-league pitcher warm up? Most of them go through an elaborate ritual. They touch an ear, a nose, the top of their cap. They have the same ability without all the rigmarole, but it makes them feel better."

"Shouldn't people feel good about themselves without a crutch?"

"Even Superman puts on a fancy suit when he flies off to save humanity."

This time she returned his smile. "You've given me something to think about."

"I hope so. You're a warm, vibrant woman, Kate. It's time you stopped trying to hide the fact, and let people get to know you."

"I'm not very experienced socially. How do you think I should act with Palmer next Saturday?" she asked anxiously. "Do men really like women who are aggressive?"

"Are you asking me how to turn a man on?" Garrett's voice lost some of its warmth.

Her color heightened, but she said lightly, "That's the advanced course. First I have to get a date with him."

"That shouldn't be a problem. He seemed quite taken with you at the reunion."

"But he never got around to asking for a date. I've read articles that say it's acceptable to offer a man your phone number, but I don't think I could do that," she said doubtfully.

"There are subtler ways."

"For instance?"

He gazed at her delicate, luminous face. "One way is to make him think you might not accept. All men want what they can't have. Palmer more than most, I'll bet," Garrett added with a touch of contempt.

Kate was too intent to defend Palmer. "If I act like I'm not interested, he's *sure* not to ask me."

"Not necessarily. He's attracted to you, and that would make you a challenge."

"It sounds awfully risky to me."

"There's another way. You could pretend to be attracted to *me*," Garrett said casually. "Palmer's very competitive. He'd be bound to rise to the bait."

"That makes more sense. But you'd have to pretend to return the interest."

"I'd be willing to make the sacrifice." He smiled.

She slanted a glance at him. "That *would* be a sacrifice. Betty has her sights set on you. Even Palmer said so."

"If the all-American boy said it, then it must be true." Garrett's voice was heavy with irony. "But it takes two to sing a duet, and I don't fool around with married women."

Kate was unaccountably happy to have her suspicions refuted. A lot of men with Garrett's looks, charm and money wouldn't be so scrupulous. He was an enigma, though.

"It's surprising that you were free two Saturday nights in a row," she remarked.

"Not free, just inexpensive." He grinned mischievously. "Which reminds me. I'll have to call Foster and have him return your check."

"It's funny the way one decision can change your whole life," she commented with a touch of wonder. "Even after I drove all the way to his agency, I almost didn't go in. I might never have met you."

"I take it you're glad you did?" Garrett asked softly.

"How can you doubt it? Look at me." She touched the shining hair that brushed her shoulders. "And this is only the beginning. I'm almost certain Palmer will ask me out."

Garrett's expression hardened. "I sure as hell hope so! It's the only way you'll ever realize your dream prince exists solely in your own mind."

"You've expressed yourself on that subject several times," she said with annoyance. "But you happen to be the only person who feels that way about him."

"Scarcely. Try asking Ken's opinion some time. Or almost anyone who meets the guy at this point in time, without all the football-hero hype."

"I can't believe you're jealous!" she exclaimed.

"Of what? A retarded adolescent who's still throwing passes?"

"Since we'll obviously never agree, let's drop the subject," she answered stiffly.

"Gladly."

Kate sneaked a look at Garrett's autocratic face. "Will you still take me to the party?"

"Sure." His mouth curved mockingly. "I'll even keep my promise to help you achieve your heart's desire."

She didn't want to talk about Palmer any more. Garrett's antipathy toward him was baffling, but it upset her when he turned cold like this. She valued his opinion on everything else.

To smooth over the awkward moment she said, "You never did tell me how I was lucky enough to catch you without a date two Saturday nights in a row."

"I was the lucky one." He smiled, his mood lightening abruptly.

"Seriously, Garrett. Don't you go with someone special?"

"I regard every woman I take out as special."

That didn't tell Kate much. "I know so little about you. You never talk about yourself."

"What would you like to know?"

"Everything. If you have any family, where you live, what you like to do in your spare time."

"I live in an apartment on Beverly Mountain Road, and I also have a beach house at Malibu. I enjoy almost any kind of sport, but I don't always have time to indulge because I often work on weekends. We're opening three new branch stores, and they take a lot of planning."

"Aren't you awfully young to be head of such a large chain?"

"Normally I wouldn't have taken over yet, but the doctor told my father to slow down or he'd be a candidate for a heart attack. I stepped in a little sooner than scheduled, that's all."

"It must have been a tremendous responsibility. Were you trained for the job?"

"From the basement up. I began working for my father during the summer, while I was still a teenager. At first I ran errands and helped out in the mail room. When I was promoted to salesclerk, I thought I was ready to take over Dad's job."

"You were obviously groomed for it. Were you the oldest son?"

"The only one. I have a sister whose husband is treasurer of the company. Trevor is a great guy, but sometimes I think . . ." His voice trailed off. After a moment he shrugged off whatever was bothering him. "Does that answer your questions?"

Not all of them. He hadn't touched on his personal life, but Kate couldn't very well ask about that. She couldn't help wondering, though. What kind of woman was Garrett attracted to? There had to be a special woman in his life, in spite of his evasiveness. Or rather, because of it. She was probably somebody ravishingly beautiful, with unlimited poise. Kate sighed unconsciously.

"Now it's your turn," he said. "Tell me about *your* life."

"You already know more than I'd prefer."

"Friends don't have to feel embarrassed with each other." He covered her hand. "You can tell me anything."

Kate's heartbeat quickened as she gazed into his deep blue eyes. Garrett was an intensely masculine man. When he was this close, turning on the full power of his charm, it was all too easy to imagine herself in his arms, with his lips moving sensuously over hers. That was *one* thing she couldn't tell him. It didn't come under the heading of friendship.

She laughed a little nervously. "Okay, I'll think of you as the big brother I always wanted."

Garrett looked back at her impassively. "Do you have sisters?"

"No, I was an only child."

"That must have been lonely."

"Not really. I was closer to my parents for being the only one. We did all kinds of exciting things together. Every year we'd go to Hawaii over the Christmas holidays with a group of their friends who had kids my age."

"That sounds like fun."

"It was." Her eyes were pensive. "I have wonderful memories of them. My parents were fun to be with."

"Did something happen to them?" he asked quietly.

"They were killed in an automobile accident the summer I graduated from junior high school."

"I'm so sorry." His voice throbbed with sympathy.

"Yes, it was tragic. They loved life so much. Dad used to say you should never put off doing the things you want to do, no matter how impractical they seem. He said old age was time enough to be conservative. But he never got old."

"It should be comforting to know he realized many of his dreams," Garrett said gently.

"It is now, but at the time I was too devastated to rationalize. I'd not only lost my whole family, I was left almost penniless. Dad made a lot of money, which we spent like tomorrow would never come. He was too young to expect to die, and he always felt invincible, anyway."

"Didn't he at least have insurance?"

"Not a great deal, and what he had went to pay outstanding debts that wouldn't have been a problem if he'd lived."

"Did you have family to go to?"

"Only an elderly great-aunt. She took me in, even though she wasn't in great financial condition herself."

"That must have been a difficult transition for you, adjusting to an older person after all the other things you'd been through."

Kate smiled for the first time. "Aunt Jen isn't your average little old lady. Her big regret in life is that she never learned to ride a motorcycle. I'm constantly terrified that one day she'll take lessons."

Garrett's eyebrows climbed. "How old is she?"

"Way up there, but she's very vague about the actual number. I once tried to find out by asking how many candles to put on her birthday cake and she said, 'Surprise me.'"

He chuckled. "I'd like to meet her. Does she live here in Los Angeles?"

"Yes, that's why I had to move here. I was born and raised in San Diego."

"You poor kid. Your whole world was turned upside down."

"It wasn't easy at first," she admitted. "Going to a new school where you don't know a soul is agonizing for a teenager. Even if I hadn't had to work after school, I'd still have felt like an outsider."

"I admire your perseverance under the circumstances. You had a goal, and you stuck to it."

"It was all I had," she answered simply. "Aunt Jen and my career."

"You're going to have a lot more from now on." Garrett's voice was husky.

"I didn't tell you all this to make you feel sorry for me," she said with dignity. "I really have a very rewarding life. Maybe I'm not as outgoing as I might have been, but now you know the reason. You tend to be a little insecure when you lose most of the people who love you."

He squeezed her hand hard. "A lot of people would love you, if you gave them a chance. The genes you inherited from your parents and Aunt Jen are there under all that reserve. We just have to scrape away the defensive layers."

"It sounds painful." She laughed.

"Trust me, honey. It won't be," he answered deeply.

Once again she'd bared her soul to Garrett, Kate thought disgustedly. Now he pitied her more than ever. If only she knew how to be bright and witty, so he'd like her for herself.

She glanced at her watch self-consciously. "My goodness, I didn't realize it was this late. I have to get home. I, uh, I'm expecting a phone call."

"I wish I could take you to dinner, but I have an appointment."

"That's perfectly all right. I didn't expect you to."

"I'd like to, though. Let's see. I have some people coming in from Seattle tomorrow. How about Thursday night?"

"No, I have to work late," she said swiftly, determined not to accept any more handouts. "Besides, I'll see you on Saturday."

"Is twice in one week too much?" He smiled.

"Three times, counting today."

His eyes wandered over her admiringly. "Today definitely counts."

Garrett went back to his office after he left Kate. Sylvia was just leaving for the day, but she lingered to brief him on a couple of things.

After delivering the messages, she said casually, "About that bill the gown shop sent up here, the one for Miss Beaumont. Should I send it to accounting?"

"Not until I adjust it. I gave her a discount."

"I can figure that for you. How much of a discount?"

"Well, actually I gave them to her below cost—and she still thought they were too expensive." Garrett laughed.

"Doesn't she know what couture costs?"

"No, and I hope to God she never finds out or I'm in deep trouble. Underneath that angelic face is a healthy temper." He was still chuckling when he went into his office to call Foster Gray.

"How was your date with the schoolmarm?" Foster asked immediately.

"Very pleasant," Garrett answered evenly.

"Will you tell me what that was all about? Why did you volunteer?"

"It seemed like the right thing to do."

"Why?"

"Because she wasn't looking for one of your studs," Garrett said tersely.

"How do you know? Maybe that's exactly what she was looking for."

"Knock it off, Foster! She told you what she wanted— a date for her high-school reunion."

"Then why didn't you let me supply one? That *is* my business."

"The less said about your business the better."

"You're part of it now, old friend," Foster chortled. "What do you think people would say about the foreman of the grand jury moonlighting as a paid escort?"

"What does my being on the grand jury have to do with anything?"

"It's practically a political job, and you know how people feel these days about a politician's morals."

"You're admitting your paid escorts are immoral?" Garrett asked ominously.

"Of course not! I was only kidding," Foster answered hastily. "It just struck me funny that one of the richest bachelors in town would pretend to be for hire. That's why I told her she couldn't afford you."

"That bit of information contributed to the merry mix-up," Garrett said dryly.

"Did you ever tell her who you really are?"

"Eventually. She was less than delighted."

"My God, what does the woman want? She got a date with a tycoon for pocket money."

"I'd scarcely call your prices small change, and that's what I called about. I want you to send her check back."

"I can't. I already deposited it."

"Then send her your own check," Garrett said impatiently.

"Do you give *your* customers their money back after they've used the merchandise? In a manner of speaking, naturally," Foster drawled mockingly.

"I don't appreciate your so-called humor. Absolutely nothing happened between Kate and me, nor did I intend for it to. I simply followed a humanitarian impulse."

"Yeah, I've followed a few of those myself, and sometimes they even work out. The repressed ones can be dynamite, once they cut loose."

Garrett lost his temper abruptly, but he didn't raise his voice. Instead it was deadly quiet. "Listen to me, Foster, because I don't intend to repeat myself. I don't give a damn what you think about me, but Kate Beaumont is the kind of woman you don't meet very often these days. She's sweet and innocent, and she'd be humiliated if this incident ever became known. If I hear that you've so much as mentioned her name, I'll break you into pieces small enough to use for toothpicks."

"Hey, lighten up, man. You know I wouldn't do anything to jeopardize our friendship."

"Then back off Kate."

"Sure, anything you say. The subject is history. How about getting together for a game of handball? This desk work is ruining my boyish figure."

"Maybe next week," Garrett answered grudgingly.

"Okay, I'll call you."

Foster stared speculatively at the phone after he'd hung up. "I never saw the guy this interested," he murmured aloud. "If everything works out, it won't hurt to remind him that I was the one responsible."

Chapter Four

The red light on Kate's answering machine was glowing when she returned from her day at the Carriage House. For a moment her eyes brightened. Maybe Garrett's appointment had been canceled and he was going to ask her out to dinner, after all.

Her hopes proved groundless. The message on the tape was from Betty. Either to call off the party or to disinvite her, Kate thought drearily. This day had had more highs and lows than the stock market.

Betty wasn't guilty of either intention, Kate discovered when she returned her call. After they'd discussed the reunion for a couple of moments Betty said, "I wanted to tell you the pool party's been changed to a barbecue. I suddenly realized nobody wants to walk around with yucky hair all night."

So much for the pink bikini, Kate thought with mixed emotions. "A barbecue sounds just as nice," she answered politely.

"I've been phoning everyone about the change in plans, but I couldn't seem to find Garrett's number in the book," Betty remarked innocently. "Can you give it to me?"

"I'll relay the message and save you a call." Kate's mouth curved cynically, knowing that wasn't what the other woman wanted.

"I think it's only polite for me to call him myself. I have a pencil and paper right here. What's his number?"

"Well, actually I never call him," Kate said truthfully. "If you can't find it in the book it must be unlisted."

Betty laughed. "I don't blame you for wanting to keep him all to yourself. He's quite a hunk."

"He's also an extremely nice person."

"Where did you meet him?" Betty asked curiously.

"I, uh, through a friend."

"What does he do for a living? I couldn't get it out of him."

"He works in his family business," Kate replied vaguely.

Betty was bound to find out who Garrett was, but she was reluctant to tell her. Betty would *really* be all over him once she found out what else he had to recommend him.

"Is his family by any chance called the Mafia?" Betty asked.

"How could you think such a thing?" Kate gasped.

"You're both so evasive whenever the subject comes up. That would certainly be one explanation. It's okay, though. You can tell me. I think it's rather exciting."

"Then you won't be too thrilled to find out he's really a shopkeeper," Kate said dryly.

"Garrett? I don't believe it! I can't see him doing anything that mundane."

"It's true. He doesn't like to talk about it, though, so it might be just as well not to mention it." Kate was careful to hide her amusement.

"I see." Betty's voice was preoccupied. "What kind of store does he have?"

"There's someone at my door, Betty," Kate said hastily. "I'll see you on Saturday."

After she hung up, Kate called Garrett at his office on the off chance that he might still be there. But the switchboard operator informed her that his secretary had gone for the day, and she refused to ring his private office.

The following day Kate tried again while she was on a coffee break. This time she got through to Garrett.

When she explained what had happened, he said, "Let me give you the number of my private line. You won't have to go through anyone else to get me. I'd also better give you my home number, since it's unlisted."

"That's what I told Betty."

"She called you for my number?"

"She *said* it was to tell you the party had been changed to a barbecue."

"But you think she had an ulterior motive." He chuckled. "You can't hold me responsible for that. If I'd had any designs on your old school chum, I would have called *her*."

"I wasn't accusing you of anything, just relaying a message." Kate was delighted with his reasoning, in spite of her claim to be nonjudgmental.

"You don't care if it's a pool party or not, do you?" he asked.

"Not really, except I bought a bikini yesterday and I was all psyched up to wear it."

"Now *I'm* disappointed."

"I probably would have chickened out at the last minute, anyway."

"You have to take the plunge. I'll tell you what. Next Sunday we'll spend the day at my place in Malibu. The Sunday after this one," he added swiftly, indicating he already had another date.

That was to be expected, but Kate was surprised to find the knowledge displeased her. Garrett had taken over her life so completely in the past few days that she'd developed a proprietary feeling toward him.

"Would you like that?" he asked when she didn't respond immediately.

"Yes, it sounds lovely."

"I don't get down there as often as I'd like. I can't guarantee what condition the place will be in," he warned.

"Are you trying to get free maid service?" she joked.

"Now you know all my secrets." He laughed.

"Speaking of secrets—I'm afraid yours is out. Or at least it will be on Saturday. Betty insisted on knowing what you do for a living."

"Why didn't you tell her? I don't have anything to hide any more."

"I did tell her . . . sort of."

"What does sort of mean?"

"I told her you were a shopkeeper."

To Kate's relief, Garrett sounded amused. "You didn't lie. That's what I am."

"Hardly. That's like saying van Gogh painted houses."

"I'd scarcely put myself in such rarefied company. Excuse me just a minute." His secretary's voice was a murmur in the background. Garrett returned to say, "I'm sorry, but my people have arrived from Seattle. I'll see you on Saturday, Kate."

Betty and Ken's home in Beverly Hills lived up to Palmer's description. A sprawling modern house was set in the middle of a spacious lawn so green and evenly mowed that it almost looked like artificial grass.

Several cars were already parked in the circular drive when Kate and Garrett arrived. A uniformed maid answered the doorbell and led them through the house to a broad flagstone terrace in back. It overlooked a kidney-shaped swimming pool that had flowers floating on the surface, along with small votive candles flickering romantically in the gathering dusk.

Betty came to welcome them, dressed in a strapless sarong-type dress that showed off her lush figure to perfection. The vibrant colors were like the plumage of some exotic bird.

Kate had been quite pleased with the white eyelet outfit she'd bought during her shopping spree. It had narrow pants and a cropped sleeveless top. She'd thought it was mildly sexy, yet casual enough for a barbecue. But Betty's glamorous outfit overshadowed hers.

"She makes me look like a bottle of milk," Kate murmured to Garrett before their hostess reached them.

He put his arm around her. "More like vanilla ice cream. Sweet and sinfully delicious."

"So good to see you again. Get yourselves a drink and mingle," Betty said. "You know most of the people here."

"You have a lovely home," Kate remarked politely.

"It's a fun place to entertain. I'll show you the tennis court later. Do you play tennis?" The question was ostensibly directed at both of them, but Betty was looking at Garrett.

"I play *at* it," he answered.

"Don't be modest." Her eyes swept his broad shoulders admiringly. "I'll bet you're good."

"He is," Kate said coolly.

Garrett's face was brimming with merriment as some new arrivals claimed Betty's attention. "Thanks for the vote of confidence. I hope I can live up to it."

Kate's cheeks colored slightly. "I was simply following our game plan."

"Weren't we supposed to put on our act in front of Palmer?" he teased.

She looked around for him. There was a group of people by the pool, and another clustered around the bar. Palmer was in the group by the bar set up at the far corner of the terrace. He had his arm around a small, curvaceous redhead.

It hadn't occurred to Kate that naturally Palmer would have a date tonight. This presented a serious setback, though. How could she play up to him under the circumstances? It probably wouldn't do any good, anyway, she thought hopelessly. He seemed very taken with the sexy redhead.

Garrett followed her gaze, assessing the situation without comment. "Shall we get a drink?" he asked.

Palmer hailed their approach. "Hi, you two. Wasn't that some bash last week?" When they agreed that it had been, he introduced his date as Barbara Portman.

"I gather you didn't go to good old Hollywood High, either," Garrett remarked to her.

"No, I went to private school," she answered.

"A girl's school, at that. She missed out on all the fun," Palmer said.

"Garrett went to a boy's school, and I don't think he felt deprived," Kate commented.

He took her hand and gazed deeply into her eyes. "Let's say I've made up for it since I met you."

"Why don't you say nice things like that to me?" Barbara pouted to Palmer.

"Knock it off, Garrett," Palmer said. "You're making the rest of us look bad."

"Is Garrett being naughty?" Betty joined them and linked her arm through his, tilting her head to smile up at him.

Palmer witnessed her behavior with a raised eyebrow. "You're collecting quite a harem," he said to Garrett.

"That's never been an ambition of mine." Garrett put his other arm around Kate and drew her close. "I'm a one-woman man."

"You mean one at a time." Palmer laughed.

"Would you want any other woman if you could have Kate?" Garrett asked without taking his eyes from hers.

"I'm about to have a saccharine attack." Betty withdrew her arm abruptly.

When Ken returned from showing a couple his prize roses, Kate and Garrett went to greet their host. The group around the bar broke up and wandered in different directions.

The cocktail hour was long. A maid passed delicious hors d'oeuvres that were largely ignored by everyone except Ken, Kate and Garrett. The rest of the guests were more interested in drinking. No one got drunk, but the level of hilarity was definitely high.

Finally Ken made a low-voiced suggestion to his wife. "Perhaps you should tell the caterer to serve dinner now."

"Don't be a party pooper," she answered. "Everyone's having a good time."

"I think they could use some food," he said mildly.

"You're being stuffy." She turned to the guests, raising her voice. "Ken says it's time to close the bar and have dinner. Is anybody hungry?"

"No!" a loud chorus greeted her.

After Betty disappeared into the house for a moment, loud music was amplified onto the terrace. Couples drifted together and started dancing.

"Should we raid the kitchen or go out for a hamburger?" Garrett asked Kate.

"I ate a lot of hors d'oeuvres. I'm not really hungry, but you must be starved."

"Not really. I thought you might be. Would you like to dance?"

As they started onto the terrace, Palmer blocked the way. "How about sharing the wealth?" he asked Garrett. "I've been waiting all night to dance with Kate."

Garrett cupped her chin in his hand and said in a deep velvet voice, "I've been waiting for her all my life."

"Then ten more minutes won't make that much difference." Palmer put his arm around Kate's waist and led her away before Garrett could object.

She knew Garrett was only playing his part in their little charade, but her skin still tingled from his touch. He must be a master at seduction when he was really in earnest.

Palmer's voice jolted her out of her reverie. "The guy really has it bad."

"Garrett is a very good friend," she said softly.

"Does that mean you see other men?"

"Rarely. Garrett doesn't like it."

"That sounds as if he's more than just a friend," Palmer persisted.

"Does it matter?"

"Strangely enough, it does. When I saw you again at the reunion, sparks flew. I felt we were on the brink of something exciting."

"You didn't even ask for my phone number."

"Everything was so hectic. We never had a moment without interruptions."

"People make time for things that are important to them," she observed.

"I knew I'd see you tonight and I promised myself I'd get you alone, one way or another." His arms tightened. "I wanted to ask you to come with me to the party, but I already had a date with Barbara, unfortunately."

"Are you going together?"

"No, she's just a girl I date now and then. There's no one special in my life."

"I can hardly believe that."

She gazed up at him, remembering how all their classmates had flocked around him at the reunion, the same way they'd heaped adulation on him in school. In a series of flashbacks she could see Palmer sauntering down the hallway, surrounded by his group of sycophants. Palmer riding in an open convertible filled with the most popular kids in school. It still didn't seem possible that she was here in his arms.

"Garrett isn't the only one who's been looking for someone special." His voice had a throb in it. "Is there a chance for me, Kate?"

It was difficult to remain aloof. "I . . . I don't know," she answered breathlessly.

"Why don't we find out?" He smiled. "How about dinner Tuesday night?"

Kate was mindful of Garrett's advice, which had worked so far. "I can't make it Tuesday." She was afraid to push her luck too far, however, so she added carelessly, "Possibly Wednesday night."

"That's great! Garrett's going to find out he's up against a real competitor."

Kate was bubbling with excitement when she rejoined Garrett a short time later. In a burst of exuberance she threw her arms around his neck.

"You're an absolute genius!" she exclaimed.

His expression was mocking as he gazed down at her glowing face. "I gather Mr. Wonderful finally succumbed to your charms."

When Garrett remained passive in her embrace, Kate removed her arms self-consciously. "Palmer asked me for a date," she said more quietly.

"Splendid. When does the big event take place?"

"Next Wednesday night."

"Congratulations. Mission accomplished."

"I know you don't like Palmer, but I thought you'd be happy for me," she said in a muted voice. "You're the one who made it all possible."

"I hope you don't hold that against me," he muttered, striding away.

Dinner was served eventually. It was a relaxed affair where everyone filled a plate from the buffet and perched on chaises around the pool or sat at several tables set up for the occasion. Kate and Garrett shared a table with Betty and Ken and another couple.

After his one outburst Garrett returned to his usual urbane self, charming everyone around him. The only difference was he didn't continue to devote himself exclusively to Kate. She realized it was no longer necessary, but she missed the warm feeling his attentiveness had given her, even knowing the reason for it.

Betty was quick to notice the change in his attitude and take advantage of it. Kate observed the two of them alone together in a dark corner of the garden at one point in the evening.

When the party was finally over, Kate approached the subject indirectly in the car going home. "Did you have a good time?" she asked.

"Not as good a time as you did," Garrett answered sardonically.

"You didn't seem to be suffering when I saw you in the garden with Betty."

"I was being polite," he answered curtly. "This was your night, but thank God you won't need me anymore."

"Won't I see you again?" she asked in a small voice.

"You'll have Palmer."

She glanced at his rugged profile, silhouetted by the dashboard lights. "I'll miss you," she said wistfully.

His face softened as he turned his head to look at her. "I'll be around."

"You mean our date next weekend is still on?" she asked hopefully.

Garrett hesitated as he drew up in front of her apartment and turned off the motor. "Maybe I'd better take a rain check on that."

"Sure." Kate tried to conceal her disappointment under a light tone. "If all goes well, I might be tied up myself."

"That's what I figured," he answered tonelessly.

They walked silently to her front door. As Kate was preparing to say a forlorn goodbye, Garrett took both her hands and held them tightly.

"I hope all your expectations are fulfilled, but if they aren't you know you can always call me."

"You needn't worry about that." She managed a tiny smile. "I appreciate what you've done for me, but I'm not going to be a millstone around your neck."

"Don't talk that way! I care about what happens to you."

"Why?" She stared up at him, seeking some clue to his feelings.

"Because you've gotten a raw deal out of life. I don't want to see you get knocked down again."

Kate had her answer. In spite of her new image, Garrett still felt sorry for her. But she was tougher than he knew. She didn't need a crutch, no matter how attractive it was.

"I'm used to fighting my own battles," she said simply. "I'll survive."

"You deserve more than that. You have a great deal to offer."

"So far I haven't found any takers, but maybe my luck is changing," she joked.

Garrett started to say something, then thought better of it. "You could be right," he said instead. "No matter what happens, just remember you're a very special person. Good night, Kate." After kissing her cheek, he left swiftly.

She went inside and walked slowly into the bedroom. But instead of getting undressed, Kate sat on the foot of the bed, trying to sort out her emotions. This should be the happiest night of her life. She'd finally gotten what Garrett called her heart's desire, and he was right. Palmer was a dream come true. Why did he have to cost her Garrett's friendship, though?

Garrett's departure would leave a gap in her life. No one had cared that much about her in a long time. She'd miss his encouragement and all the attention that had made her feel desirable. Garrett was an outstanding man in every way. Even though Palmer represented everything she'd pined for, Kate could still appreciate Garrett's potent appeal. What woman could be indifferent to that rugged face and fantastic body?

With a sigh, she stood up and started to get undressed.

Kate's spirits were considerably brighter the next morning when excitement over her date with Palmer began to grow. As the days passed, her anticipation mounted, along with her nervousness. She longed for one of Garrett's pep talks, then told herself to stop acting like a teenager. Palmer wouldn't be interested in her if she wasn't a poised, intelligent woman.

Kate had purchased all the cosmetics Caroline had used to make up her face. After much practice she'd learned to duplicate the result herself. But for the most important night of her life she decided to put herself in the hands of professionals. She made a late-afternoon appointment for Wednesday at the Carriage House beauty salon.

Their magic didn't take as long this time because her hair didn't require cutting or a color rinse. Even so, Kate was shocked when she paid her bill. She didn't want to think what the first visit had cost!

It suddenly occurred to her that she'd never thanked Garrett for that. As long as she was right there in the store, it seemed the courteous thing to do. She wasn't inventing excuses to see him again, Kate assured herself, only showing good manners.

Garrett's secretary was polite, but doubtful about the wisdom of her unscheduled visit. "Mr. Richmond has someone in his office right now. I can't tell you how long he'll be, but you can wait if you like."

Kate sat in the reception room, having second thoughts about her impulsive decision when she observed the bustle all around her. Garrett didn't have time for the amenities during his busy working day. He might even get the wrong idea about why she'd come.

Standing abruptly, Kate went back to Sylvia's office. "I've decided not to wait, after all," she told the woman.

"I'm sorry, Miss Beaumont. Can I give him any message?"

"No thanks, it wasn't important. As a matter of fact, you don't even have to tell him I was here."

"I'm sure he'd want—" Sylvia paused as the door to Garrett's office opened.

Garrett shook hands with his departing visitor, then glimpsed Kate standing by the desk. "Kate! This is a nice surprise." He smiled at her.

"I just stopped by to thank you for . . . I mean, I was downstairs, and . . ."

"Come into my office."

After he'd closed the door she mumbled, "You're busy. I shouldn't have bothered you."

"Never too busy for you. What can I do for you?"

"You've already done it. After I had my hair styled just now, I realized how much Philippe charges."

"He's worth it." Garrett assessed her gleaming hair.

"I suppose you should expect to pay for miracles." She smiled.

He leaned against the desk and folded his arms across his broad chest. "Tonight's the big night, isn't it?"

"Yes."

"Would you like to have a drink to celebrate?"

"I don't have time," she answered reluctantly after a glance at her watch.

The mocking smile she hated curved his mouth. "I wouldn't want to make you late for the date of the century."

Kate realized what a mistake it had been to come. "Goodbye, Garrett. I'm sorry I disturbed you." She left without waiting for a reply.

Alone in his office he stared at the closed door and murmured, "More than you know."

Kate was ready and waiting when Palmer arrived. She'd sprayed herself with perfume, checked her appearance half a dozen times and taken deep breaths to conquer her nervousness.

What Palmer noticed most was her curved figure in the clinging, moss-green silk dress. "You look delicious!" His eyes glowed as he prowled around her.

"Thank you." She fiddled with the low neckline of her dress, hiking it up a fraction of an inch. "Would you like a drink?"

"We'll get one at the restaurant."

"All right, I'll get my coat."

After helping her on with her wrap, he nuzzled her neck with his lips. "Mmm, you smell luscious, too. This is going to be a night to remember."

"Yes, it is," she agreed faintly.

He squeezed her hand. "Come on. Let's get dinner out of the way."

Kate was thrilled by his admiration, yet disturbed by his aggressiveness on a first date. Then she reminded herself that Palmer considered them old friends.

His behavior was more restrained in the restaurant, a currently popular spot named L'Auberge. It was filled with an assured, well-dressed crowd. Although Palmer had made reservations, they were kept waiting at the bar for almost half an hour.

"Have you been here before?" he asked her.

"No, but I've heard good things about it."

"The food will be worth the wait. If we ever get seated." He frowned.

"We're not in a hurry," she said soothingly.

"No, but it fries me when people take a reservation and then don't honor it."

"Judging by the name, I suppose they specialize in French cuisine," she remarked to distract him.

"That's right, but I'll bet every town in America has a restaurant named L'Auberge. Some of them probably serve Chinese food."

"I guess it's as valid as calling a restaurant an inn."

"Is that what *auberge* means?"

She smiled. "Didn't you pay attention in French class?"

"I didn't have to. Old lady Dampierre couldn't very well flunk the captain of the football team."

"You still remember her name," Kate exclaimed.

"I haven't forgotten anything about high school. Those were the best years of my life."

"How about college?"

"It wasn't the same." A discontented look crossed his handsome face. "Who wants to be an insignificant cog in a big, impersonal machine?"

"It's hard to go from being a senior to a freshman again, but I don't imagine you went unnoticed for long."

"Long enough," he said tersely. "I quit after a year."

Remembering how she'd struggled for her own education, Kate couldn't help expressing her disapproval. "You didn't give college much of a chance."

"What was the point? They don't let you play football until your junior year. I was just wasting time. Besides, I got a great opportunity to go into a top brokerage office. I'll bet I'm making more money today than those guys who stuck around for a degree."

Palmer's name was called over the loudspeaker and they went into the dining room where the headwaiter led them to a table.

By the time they'd made their selections from the large menu and given their order, Kate had gotten over her slight disappointment in Palmer. When the waiter had gone he held her hands across the table and gazed deeply into her eyes.

"You certainly grew up to be a pretty girl," he murmured.

"Meaning there was a lot of room for improvement?" she teased.

"You know I didn't mean it that way."

"It's all right. I *have* changed. I'm a scientist now," she said with quiet pride.

"You're kidding!"

"No. I work for the Strawbridge Research Institute."

"You dissect frogs and things like that?"

"Not exactly." She laughed. "I'm a microbiologist."

"How did a nice girl like you get mixed up with a bunch of germs?"

"That's a common misconception. We actually deal with microscopic forms of life."

"You're adorable. Do you know that?"

"It isn't mentioned much around the lab," she answered dryly.

"I'm going to mention it often." His voice deepened. "You hit me like a ton of bricks at the reunion. I have a feeling you're going to become a very important part of my life."

Kate had been a little hurt that he wasn't more interested in her work, but Palmer's declaration drove his indifference out of her mind. Could he possibly mean what he'd said?

"Unless Garrett has the inside track," he added casually. "You're not just stringing me along, are you, Kate?"

"No!" she gasped. "Garrett and I are merely good friends. I mean, I'm very fond of him, but we haven't made any commitment." That was close enough to the truth.

"I'll bet he feels differently, but that's his tough luck," Palmer said with satisfaction.

When the waiter brought their food, Kate's pulse quieted down. They discussed everyday things, restaurants they'd been to and movies they'd seen. Palmer also talked about his work, becoming very animated. Kate was enthralled. Not so much by the stock market as by the fact that Palmer seemed totally engrossed in her. By telling her all his hopes and ambitions, he proved she was special to him.

It was almost ten-thirty before they finished dinner. As they drove away from the restaurant Palmer suggested an after-dinner drink.

"Don't stockbrokers on the west coast have to get up terribly early?" Kate asked.

"I don't need much sleep," he assured her. "Sometimes I stay up all night, go to work and then crash in the afternoon."

"I can't sleep in the daytime. It's too noisy."

"That's the beauty of having a corner apartment—no neighbors on two sides. We'll have a drink at my place and you'll see how private it is."

Kate wasn't entirely comfortable with the idea, but she didn't like to say anything. The days when a nice girl didn't go to a man's apartment were as antiquated as lace valentines. Palmer would surely tease her unmercifully.

He lived in a beautiful building in a good part of town, but his apartment was small. Or maybe it was all the exercise equipment that crowded the starkly modern living room.

"I keep the bedroom clear for more important activities." He winked at her as he turned on the stereo and opened the doors of a mirrored cabinet. "What would you like to drink?"

She perched gingerly on a white leather couch. "Whatever you're having."

"Coming right up." He handed her a small glass of milky liquid.

She tasted it and made a face. "What is this stuff?"

"It's supposed to be an aphrodisiac, but I think the claim is overrated." He smiled a little lewdly. "Maybe because I've never needed one."

Kate walked over and put her glass on the bar. "I hope you don't mind if I skip the drink. This must be an acquired taste."

He drew her into his arms and moved slowly to the syrupy music filling the room. "I'll bet you don't need an aphrodisiac, either."

She tried to pull away. "I think I'd like to go home now, Palmer."

"You don't mean that. The evening is just starting to get interesting, sweet thing." His hand curved around her breast, as he rotated his hips suggestively against hers.

"Stop it, Palmer!" she demanded sharply, struggling to free herself.

"You don't have to put on an act. I could tell at the reunion that you had the hots for me."

"You're wrong!"

"Oh, yeah?" He chuckled. "Even your boyfriend could tell. He was plenty jealous."

"That wasn't the reason Garrett disliked you," she said scornfully.

"He knew he was outclassed," Palmer crowed. "After tonight you can tell him who's the better man."

Kate felt a shiver of revulsion as his wet mouth closed over hers. The disgust mounted when his groping hands wandered over her body. She managed to put a small distance between them, but he jerked her back and slid one hand under the hem of her dress. Out of sheer instinct she raised her knee and dug it into his groin. Palmer released her with an outcry of pain.

"You little hellcat! What do you think you're doing?" His face was contorted with anger.

She backed away, straightening her dress. "I told you to leave me alone."

"You put out for Garrett, and you can damn well put out for me," he grated. "What the hell did you think I brought you here for?"

"Certainly not for this."

"Girls like you are just asking for trouble. You give a guy a big come-on, and then pretend you didn't mean it."

"I never gave you the impression that I had anything like this in mind."

"Oh no? You couldn't take your eyes off me at the reunion. Do you think I didn't notice?"

"I had a crush on you in high school," she said quietly. "I guess a little of the stardust remained. I was excited when you remembered me and asked me out."

"I wouldn't have known you without your name tag," he answered brutally. "And none of the old crowd remembers you, either. I asked you out because you're a sexy-looking babe and I thought we could have some fun, but I don't have to work this hard for it."

"I'm sorry if I spoiled your evening," she said witheringly.

"We could salvage it." He missed the sarcasm as his eyes crawled over her consideringly. "We had a couple of misunderstandings, but we can start over again." He walked toward her with a smile that was more of a leer. "I have an old high-school jersey in the bedroom. How about a little game of touch football?"

"You couldn't have been like this in high school," she whispered, trying to find some trace of the Palmer she remembered so romantically.

"I like to think I've gotten better," he smirked.

When he reached for her, Kate shrank away. Whirling around she raced out the front door and down the hall. Without waiting for the elevator, she ran down the steps. Her heart was pounding when she reached the lobby, but she continued up the street to a hotel where several taxis were waiting for fares.

"Are you okay?" the driver asked after she'd gotten into his cab and gasped out her address.

"I will be," she answered, breathing heavily.

He noted her disheveled hair in the rearview mirror. "Date gone sour, huh?"

"Something like that."

"Well, hang in there. You know that old saying. You have to kiss a lot of frogs before you find a prince."

Her dream prince had never existed, Kate thought bitterly. Garrett was right again.

Chapter Five

Garrett was sitting in his car across from Kate's apartment, when the taxi drove up and let her off. He'd been waiting there for over an hour, hoping he was on a fool's errand. One glimpse of Kate told him he wasn't. After the cab had driven away, Garrett got out of his car and followed her into the building.

Kate didn't bother to turn on the lights. She sank down on a chair in the living room, feeling completely drained. The pain would come later, without any doubt, but for the moment she was mercifully numb. The doorbell ripped through her torpor, throwing her into a panic. She couldn't survive another scene with Palmer!

"Go away," she ordered through the closed door.

"Let me in, Kate," Garrett's voice answered. "I want to talk to you."

The thought of facing Garrett was almost as stressful. "I was in bed. I'm not dressed."

"I know you just got home."

He must have seen her arrive by taxi. That was the final degradation. Her eyes filled with tears. "Leave me alone. I don't want to see anybody right now."

"I'm not leaving." His voice was adamant.

Frustration washed over her as she was forced to open the door. Garrett wouldn't care if he roused the neighbors. "You had no right to spy on me," she raged.

"I wasn't spying. I thought you might need someone to talk to."

"Oh, sure! What you really wanted was to gloat. Well, go ahead! Take your usual shots at the all-American hero. You were right. Is that what you want to hear?" Kate's slender body was as taut as a violin string.

"I wish I'd been wrong," he said regretfully. "Would you like to tell me about it?"

"No, but that won't stop you from worming the story out of me," she answered scathingly.

"Just tell me one thing. He didn't hurt you, did he?"

"Not where it shows." She turned away.

Garrett's hands bit into her shoulders as he forced her to face him. "What are you saying? I'll kill him if he—"

"He didn't. Palmer doesn't like to work that hard. He told me so, along with a few other choice bits of information," she said in a flat voice.

"Surely you didn't believe anything he said. The man is a troglodyte!"

Kate wasn't listening. "He didn't even remember me. None of them did. I sat in the same classroom with all those people, and I might as well have been invisible."

"That was a long time ago. You're a different person now."

"I'm the same misfit, trying to kid myself that an expensive gown and a fancy hairdo will fool people."

He shook her slightly. "Forget about Palmer and the rest. You're worth more than the whole lot. Any man with an IQ higher than an eggplant would see what a warm, wonderful woman you are."

"Give it up, Garrett," she said wearily. "Palmer was only interested in getting me into bed. He wasn't even subtle about it."

"Not all men are like that. You need to meet the kind who will appreciate you as a person."

She turned away and went to stare out at the darkened street. "They'd only bother with me for the same thing. I tried to talk to Palmer about my work, and he didn't even pretend to listen."

"Palmer again!" With a sigh of exasperation, Garrett went around the room switching on all the lamps.

Kate wrapped her arms around her body, feeling exposed in the sudden light. "Why did you do that? Turn them off."

"No. It's time you came out of the shadows. Sit down, Kate. We have to do something about this monumental misconception you have of yourself."

"I've heard enough of your pitying platitudes."

"I'm through talking. Now I intend to demonstrate."

He pushed her gently onto the couch and stood over her. "Next Saturday night you're coming with me to a dance at my country club. If a number of men don't try to take you away from me, I'll agree that you're hopelessly undesirable and I'll leave you alone from then on."

"Don't you ever learn? You got Palmer to take me out, and look what happened."

"Some of the men you meet will undoubtedly want to make love to you. I do, myself," Garrett said calmly.

She gave him a startled look. "You're just saying that."

"My dear Kate, nothing would give me greater pleasure. I'd like to hold you in my arms and kiss away every tear you've ever shed."

"Because you feel sorry for me," she said dully.

With an impatient exclamation he pulled her to her feet and into his arms. Kate stiffened at the contact with his hard body, but before she could voice a protest, his mouth covered hers. Garrett's kiss was wildly different from Palmer's. His lips were firm yet gentle, bringing her much pleasure.

Her taut body gradually relaxed against his as he slowly stroked the tense muscles at her nape. Without conscious intention, her arms crept around his neck. Garrett's embrace tightened for a moment before he put her away gently.

He smoothed her rumpled hair as she stared up at him in a daze. "That should convince you that pity has nothing to do with my desire for you. I won't repeat the demonstration, but for your own good you'd better learn how you affect men."

Kate gazed at him in bemusement. If Garrett was experiencing anything like the glow she was feeling, how could he say he wasn't going to kiss her again?

"The men I introduce you to might try to go further," he was continuing dispassionately. "But I guarantee it won't be the crude assault you were subjected to tonight. A real man accepts a lady's refusal. I will warn you if I think any of them is a borderline case. This time I expect you to take my advice."

Garrett kept telling her she was desirable, but evidently not to him. "I'm sorry to disappoint you, but I refuse to be dragged into another world where I don't belong," she said coldly.

"What do you intend to do, Kate? Retire from the human race? I didn't realize you were a coward?"

His mild contempt stung. "What's so brave about going to a country-club dance?"

"Exactly. It's no big deal, so why not humor me? If you're uncomfortable, I'll take you home immediately."

"I really don't want to go," she said plaintively.

"I know." He smiled. "But you might be pleasantly surprised."

"I don't suppose you're going to give up. Do you always get your own way?"

His expression was enigmatic as he gazed at her delicate features. "When it's something I especially want."

"I wish I could say the same." She sighed.

"You don't know what you want yet."

"I thought it was Palmer, but you were right about him on every point. What really hurt was discovering that winning out over *you* was as important to him as sleeping with *me*."

"The man is obviously a mental case."

"But I didn't see it." Kate's face was troubled. "How can I be such a bad judge of character?"

"You had stardust in your eyes, but they're clear now. When the right man comes along you'll recognize him."

She smiled for the first time. "I'd be better off letting you pick one out for me."

Something flickered in his eyes as he returned her smile. "That's really what I had planned all along. Are you okay now?"

She nodded. "Thanks to you."

"Then I'd better let you get to sleep." At the door he leaned down and kissed her cheek. "Sweet dreams, little one."

Kate got undressed slowly, trying to sort out her feelings toward Garrett. Gratitude was one, certainly. He was always there with a comforting shoulder to cry on, or a compliment when she was down. But that stirring kiss went way beyond friendship—at least for her. Kate's heart beat faster when she remembered Garrett's mouth moving sensuously over hers, and the seductive feeling of his lithe body pressed closely.

Was the reaction he caused only the normal one any woman would have toward a superb male? Kate hoped so, because Garrett was only marginally attracted to her. It would be disastrous to fall in love with him. He would break her heart. Without meaning to, but that wouldn't make the pain any less. She mustn't allow herself to think of him romantically.

Kate's resolution didn't govern her subconscious. Dreams of Garrett brought a blissful smile to her face.

Garrett phoned early the next day while she was getting dressed. "How are you feeling this morning?" he asked.

"Like I'm going to make it."

"I never doubted that for a minute," he answered warmly.

"Don't you have to work today?"

"I'm on my way out the door. I couldn't remember whether I told you it's formal Saturday night. My sister taught me that women like to know these things far in advance."

"I don't know if I have anything suitable," Kate said doubtfully.

"Didn't you buy any evening clothes on your shopping spree?"

"No. I tried them on, but I didn't really have any use for them."

"Well, now you do. I'll check with Rosemary and have her send something out to you."

"Wait, Garrett! I think I can manage to find something in my closet." But it was too late. He'd already hung up.

Kate had real reservations about spending a lot of money on a dress she'd probably only wear once. But when she took it out of the large pink-and-gray Carriage House box, her conservatism vanished. It was the chiffon gown with the sequined jacket.

As she twirled in front of the mirror that Saturday night waiting for Garrett to arrive, Kate felt like a different person. She looked tall, chic and sophisticated. The daring slit in the skirt showed provocative glimpses of her long legs, and the contrast between the glittering sequined top and the soft chiffon skirt was a masterpiece of design.

Garrett's reaction on seeing her was very satisfactory. His eyes lit up as he gazed at her. "I'll be lucky if I get even one dance with you."

"I hope you won't be disappointed." Insecurity plagued her.

"The best thing that could happen would be to have you all to myself."

"That isn't what you want, though," she fretted.

"Come along, Kate. Tonight you're going to get what *you* want."

The Fair Oaks clubhouse was already crowded when they got there. A spacious lobby was filled with beautifully dressed couples, the men in stark black-and-white, a stunning foil for the brilliant gowns on the women. A steady buzz of conversation and laughter almost drowned out the music coming from a room beyond. Everyone seemed to know one another.

Kate felt her nerves tightening in a familiar way. How had she let Garrett talk her into this? He sensed her uneasiness and clasped her hand as he nodded to friends and returned greetings.

"We're sitting with my sister and her husband," Garrett said. "They're probably here already. Sharon is almost compulsively prompt."

"I'm looking forward to meeting your sister," Kate said politely, although she wasn't.

"Don't be turned off by her bossiness." He grinned. "She's really a good kid."

Their progress across the lobby was slow because Garrett was stopped often by friends. Kate acknowledged the stream of introductions stiffly, painfully aware of being under scrutiny. The women were especially sharp-eyed when Garrett draped his arm casually around her shoulders. That made her feel even more of a fraud.

They were almost to the door of the dining room when they came face-to-face with Foster Gray. It was ironic that he was the one person there whom Kate knew, yet the one she least wanted to see.

"I thought we were going to get together for a game of handball," he said genially to Garrett.

"I've been rather busy," Garrett answered.

"If your time's been taken up by this lovely lady, I definitely can't compete. Aren't you going to introduce me?"

"You've already met," Garrett said evenly. "This is Kate Beaumont."

Foster looked at her curiously. "You must be mistaken. I could never forget such a—" He broke off suddenly as the name stirred his memory. "Not the girl who—"

Kate wanted to die on the spot and become invisible, but Garrett was looking at the other man impassively. "It isn't necessary to mention the circumstances to anybody. I believe we discussed that."

"Right you are." Foster was staring at her with incredulity. "I never would have recognized you."

"We're on our way to our table," Garrett remarked.

"I'll see you later. Save me a dance," Foster said to Kate.

As they walked away she said to Garrett, "That was probably the most embarrassing thing that ever happened to me. Why did you have to tell him who I was? He said himself he never would have guessed."

"He might have at some point in the evening. I didn't want him to blurt it out inadvertently."

"Are you sure he won't tell people anyway? It makes a great story, if you're not one of the participants," she said ruefully.

"Don't worry about Foster. I let him know I'd be displeased if it got around."

"Is that enough to stop him? Sometimes even a friend can't resist a good joke."

"Besides being a friend, Foster has a remarkably well-developed instinct for where his best interests lie," Garrett said dryly.

"What could you do to him?"

"It's what I *wouldn't* do. I'm his personal bank."

"You mean he borrows money from you?"

"That's an oversimplification, but it will do."

"Garrett! Over here." An attractive young woman with short black hair was waving at him from a nearby table.

Kate could tell this was Garrett's sister. They had the same deep blue eyes fringed by black lashes, and the same classic features. The man sitting next to her wasn't as strikingly handsome, but he had an interesting face and an engaging smile.

Garrett led Kate over and introduced her. "My sister, Sharon Hamilton, and her husband, Trevor."

While the introductions were being made, Sharon inspected Kate with lively interest. "I'm glad to see my brother's taste is improving," she said to Kate.

"Cherish the compliment," he advised. "Sharon hasn't approved of anyone I've dated since Mary Jane Wilkerson in the tenth grade."

"She was the only one who knew the global-warming trend wasn't a new rock group," Sharon replied.

"I don't think Kate is interested in my teenage follies." Garrett glanced around. "We need a drink. If you see a waiter, flag him down."

"They're scarcer than affordable housing. You'll have better luck going to the bar and getting your own," Sharon advised.

"I'll go with you," Trevor offered. "We're ready for a refill."

Sharon watched her husband and brother walk away, talking easily together. "It's nice when the two men in your life get along so well," she remarked.

"They work together, too, don't they?" Kate asked.

Sharon nodded. "I think Garrett was the reason Trevor finally agreed to take the job. It was the sensible thing to do, but his regard for Garrett was the deciding factor."

"Did your husband work for a rival store?"

"No, he was creative director for a top advertising agency."

"That was quite a career change. I believe Garrett said he's now the treasurer of your company."

"Trevor has an unexpected aptitude for figures. People might think he got the job through nepotism, but it isn't true. He's very good at what he does. Garrett would never tolerate incompetence, especially from a relative."

"Or anyone else," Kate answered ironically. "He expects everyone to be as capable as he is."

Sharon laughed. "Has my brother the dictator been trying to run your life?"

"How did you guess?"

"It takes one to know one." Sharon gazed at Kate speculatively. "He must be really interested in you. Garrett is only tough on people he cares about."

Kate wanted to think that was true, but she knew differently. "He's gotten used to giving orders, that's all. We don't even know each other very well."

"How did you meet?"

"Through a misunderstanding actually. I, uh, mistook him for someone else, and we sort of got acquainted."

"That sounds intriguing."

Kate tried to head her off from pursuing the subject. "How did you meet Trevor?"

"In the usual way. Through mutual friends."

"Do you have any children?"

"Not yet. We both want a family, but I prefer to wait a while. We've only been married for two years."

Remembering the relatively short time she'd had with her own parents, Kate remarked somberly, "Sometimes it's better not to put things off."

"You sound like Trevor," Sharon answered impatiently.

"He doesn't agree with you?"

"My husband is a darling man and I adore him, but he's completely impractical. Either he rushes into things without thinking them out, or he sets his heels and resists any kind of change."

Kate smiled. "At least he isn't boring."

"No, he's never that," Sharon answered softly.

From the tender look on her face, Kate could tell Garrett's sister was very much in love with her husband. The three of them seemed like such a happy family. Did they realize how fortunate they were? she wondered wistfully.

The men returned with a drink in each hand. "Has Sharon been telling you about my sterling qualities?" Garrett asked Kate as he set her glass on the table.

"Which one was that?" Sharon teased.

"A lot of help *you* are," he complained. "I counted on you to make me look good."

"He's really awfully nice," Sharon assured Kate. "All the women are crazy about him."

"You don't have to overdo it," Garrett said mildly.

"She'll find out for herself." Sharon turned to Kate. "A couple of women here tonight will be very jealous of you."

"Would you care to dance?" Garrett asked Kate abruptly.

After they'd gone, Sharon said to her husband, "Wait until Lorna sees Kate. She's going to erupt higher than Mount Vesuvius."

"Lorna must know Garrett takes out other women."

"He's never brought them here to the club, though. That must mean he's interested enough in Kate to risk a donnybrook with Lorna," Sharon said thoughtfully.

"Or maybe it's just a date. Why do women blow everything out of proportion?" Trevor asked impatiently.

"For the same reason men can't see what's perfectly obvious," she countered.

Something flickered in Trevor's eyes as he gazed at his wife. "They don't have a corner on that failing."

"Whatever is that supposed to mean?"

His mouth curved in a lopsided smile. "Just a feeble defense. Come on, let's dance."

As Kate and Garrett circled the crowded floor she said, "Your sister is very much like you."

"Is that good or bad?" He smiled.

"Are you looking for more compliments?"

"You've never given me one."

"That's not true. I've told you lots of times how grateful I am to you."

"Gratitude is something you offer up when you don't get audited by the IRS."

"You insist on a compliment?"

"Not if you feel obligated."

"All right." She paused to consider. "I've never met a man like you. You're handsome, charming and rich. You have it all, so you might be excused for being complacent. But instead, you're the kindest person I've ever known." She gazed up at him. "Does that satisfy you?"

"I was only joking," he protested. "I don't deserve all that."

"Don't be modest, too," she teased. "That would make you insufferably perfect."

Garrett's fingertips outlined the curve of her cheek in a feathery caress. "You're much closer to that description than I am."

"Garrett, darling!" a female voice trilled suddenly. "I didn't expect to see you here tonight."

"Hello, Lorna, Freddy." Garrett nodded to the man she was dancing with. "Quite a mob scene, isn't it?"

Lorna looked pointedly at Kate. "Aren't you going to introduce us?" she asked Garrett. After he'd complied, she said to Kate, "Are you new in town? I've never seen you here before."

"This is my first time," Kate answered. "It's a lovely club."

"All of our crowd practically live here. Are you a golfer or a tennis player?"

"Neither, I'm afraid," Kate answered.

"You won't last long with Garrett, then." Lorna uttered a merry laugh. "He's a terribly physical man," she said, slanting him a meaningful look.

"I'm sure Kate doesn't need to play games to keep a man interested," Freddy observed gallantly.

"I couldn't have said it better myself," Garrett remarked. "See you both later."

The furious look on Lorna's face spoke volumes. "She must be one of the women your sister warned me about," Kate said when they'd danced away.

"Sharon talks too much," he answered curtly.

Kate didn't heed the autocratic look on his face. "Do you see a lot of Lorna?"

"Does it matter?"

"I just wondered how much trouble you're in."

"Suppose you let me worry about that."

From the grim look on his face, Kate assumed he was regretting his decision to bring her to the dance. But no more than she regretted her own weakness in coming. Lorna's reference to *their* crowd was a reminder that Kate didn't belong. How many times did she have to hear it before it sank in?

When he felt her draw away imperceptibly, Garrett glanced at her shadowed face. Putting aside his momentary annoyance he said, "Let's go to the bar. It's getting too crowded in here."

A cluster of people, mostly men, were standing along the length of a long mahogany bar in the paneled lounge. They watched Kate's approach with male interest, then greeted Garrett and made room at the bar.

"I saved this chair just for you," a blond man with a mustache told Kate as he slid off a stool.

She was immediately surrounded. Garrett introduced the three men closest to her as Chris, Mitch and Ian. They were all in their early thirties.

Ian was the easiest to remember, because he was the one with the blond hair and mustache. But Kate had trouble telling the other two apart, since both were conventionally attractive.

"Why does Garrett always get the most beautiful women?" Ian complained.

"Tell me you're not deeply involved with him," Mitch pleaded with Kate.

"Well . . . no," she answered haltingly.

"Fantastic! Prepare for some serious competition," Mitch told Garrett.

"I fully expected it." Garrett smiled. "What man could hope to keep such loveliness all to himself?"

"Then you won't mind if Kate and I have this dance," Ian said.

"That's the lady's decision, not mine."

"May I have the honor?" Ian asked formally.

Kate didn't know how to refuse. This was obviously what Garrett wanted, but these men were overwhelming. She didn't know what to say to them. Garrett thought their attention would give her confidence, but it was having the opposite effect.

"Save the next dance for me," Mitch called as they walked away.

"Garrett's a very good sport," Ian said, taking her in his arms on the dance floor. "I wouldn't give you up this easily."

"We're just good friends," she mumbled.

"That must be your choice not his, but I'm delighted to hear it. I hope it means there's room in your life for me."

"We just met," she said helplessly.

"Am I coming on too strong? I don't mean to. It's a matter of expediency. Those wolves back there are just waiting for a chance to close in."

"I gather you don't see many new faces around here," Kate remarked.

"Not like yours. But you already know that. I suppose you're dated up until Halloween."

"I wouldn't say that," she answered noncommittally.

"When can I see you then? You name the day."

Kate looked at him curiously. Ian was nice-looking and self-assured. He must be a very eligible bachelor. "Your social life can't be that limited."

"For a date with you, I'll switch things around if I have to."

She could hardly believe he was serious. A terrible thought occurred to her. "Do you and Garrett have some kind of arrangement?"

"About what?" His blank look was genuine.

For the first time, Kate felt a heady sense of power. This attractive man was practically pleading with her for a date!

"Are you worried about the ethics of making a date with me while you're out with Garrett?" Ian asked. "If it will make you feel better, I'll phone you tomorrow. Just promise you'll save me a night."

"I don't suppose Garrett would mind, since we're only friends."

"That's great! When can I see you and where would you like to go? Dancing? The theater?"

When Ian brought Kate back to the bar, Mitch and then Chris claimed her for a dance. Garrett watched with an almost paternal smile on his face.

Eventually Sharon and Trevor came looking for him. "So this is where you are," Sharon exclaimed. "I saw Kate dancing with everyone but you."

"She's having a good time," Garrett answered indulgently.

"What happened? Did you have an argument?"

"Not at all."

"You enjoy sitting here alone while the best-looking guys in the club are romancing your date?"

Garrett smiled broadly. "As a matter of fact, I'm enjoying myself very much."

"Take away his car keys, Trevor. My brother is either drunk or crazy."

"Have you ever known me to be out of control?" Garrett asked.

"I think I'm beginning to get it," Sharon said. "You brought Kate tonight to make Lorna jealous."

"Where did you get a wild idea like that?" Annoyance replaced the smile on his face.

"What other explanation is there?"

"Why do you need one? Don't you have enough to do running your own life and Trevor's?"

She raised her eyebrows. "Well, if you're going to get huffy about it. I was only showing a little sisterly concern."

"It's misplaced. Everything is fine, believe me. I knew Kate would get a big whirl, and I don't mind. But it has nothing to do with Lorna."

"Now that you know Garrett isn't feeling any pain, let's go back to the table." Trevor acted in his usual role of peacemaker.

"I'll go with you." Garrett turned to Ian. "Tell Chris to bring Kate back to our table when they finish dancing."

As the three of them walked back to the dining room, they met Lorna and Freddy.

After discovering Kate was absent, Lorna said, "You haven't danced with me all evening, Garrett."

"Freddy has a prior claim," he answered.

"Don't be silly. We're all good friends. You don't mind do you, darling?" she asked her date. Before he could express an opinion, she took Garrett's hand and pulled him toward the dance floor.

"Is Kate the reason you've been breaking dates with me lately?" she asked as they circled the floor.

"I only broke one date," he answered evasively. "The following Saturday was a misunderstanding."

"And this one?"

Garrett suppressed a sigh. "We didn't have a date."

"It was always understood that Saturday was our night."

"Evidently not, or you wouldn't be here with Freddy," he said dryly.

"You can't expect me to sit home waiting for you to call," she flared.

"I don't. You're perfectly justified in making your own plans."

"You know that's not what I want." She trailed her fingers up and down his nape. "What happened to us, Garrett? We were so happy together."

"We had fun," he corrected her carefully.

"We had more than that going for us," she declared. "You've often said you're interested in going into politics someday. I'd be the perfect partner for you. I know how to entertain, how to talk to important people. We could have such an exciting life together!"

"Are you looking for a husband or a career?" he asked ironically.

She quickly masked her chagrin. "That's unkind. You must know how I feel about you, Garrett."

"I think I've always known," he answered evenly. "Take my advice and marry Freddy. You might not get to Washington, but he'll give you everything else you want."

"Are you telling me it's over between us?" she demanded.

"What's the point in dragging it out to the bitter end, Lorna? If we call it off now, we can remain friends."

"How naive can you get?" she snapped.

"I'm sorry you feel that way."

"Just tell me one thing. What does she have that I don't?"

"Kate has nothing to do with us," he answered patiently.

"Oh, sure! And the Easter bunny lays hard-boiled eggs in pastel colors."

"I'll take you back to Freddy," Garrett said quietly.

"Wait!" She twined her arms around his neck. "Tell me what you see in her. You owe me that much."

His face softened as he gazed down at Lorna, seeing Kate instead. "How can you explain intangibles like grace and charm?"

Kate was laughing at something Chris had said. Her face sobered as she glanced over his shoulder and saw Garrett gazing at Lorna. His expression told her all she needed to know about his feelings for the other woman. Kate had guessed as much, so she couldn't understand the sharp stab of pain it caused.

"I'm sorry," she mumbled as she missed a step.

"My fault," Chris said gallantly. "You could never make a mistake."

"I might have made a monumental one," she answered sadly.

Garrett and his family were seated at the table when Chris reluctantly delivered Kate and departed.

Sharon gave her a decidedly unfriendly look. "We thought you forgot who you came with," she remarked acidly.

"That was only my sister's opinion. Did you enjoy yourself?" Garrett murmured in Kate's ear as he stood up to pull out her chair.

"Oh, yes! I have so much to tell you. You were right."

"Trust me." He pinched her chin gently between his thumb and forefinger. "I know you better than you know yourself."

Sharon watched the look that passed between them with total mystification. "Do you know what's going on?" she muttered to her husband.

Trevor smiled. "Not all the subplots, but I can get the gist of the story."

Kate tried to soothe Sharon's ruffled feathers, realizing she was only miffed on her brother's behalf. Sharon didn't know Garrett had orchestrated the evening.

"This is a lovely club," Kate remarked politely to the Hamiltons. "You must get a lot of pleasure out of it."

"I'm here more than Trevor is," Sharon answered, accepting Kate's overture.

"You don't care for sports?" Kate asked him.

"My wife and brother-in-law are the competitive ones in the family," he replied with a faint smile.

"Garrett was the club golf champion a few years ago," Sharon told Kate proudly. "He could be again if he had more time to play."

"I'm not surprised. Garrett is good at everything." This time Kate wasn't merely being polite.

"Don't you think you should sample all of my talents before you make such a sweeping statement?" he teased.

As her color rose, Trevor took pity on her. "Do you play golf, Kate?"

"No. I grew up in San Diego where we did more swimming and sailing."

"We have an Olympic-size pool here at the club. Maybe you can have lunch with me one day and go for a swim," Sharon suggested.

"I'd like that, but I work during the week."

"What do you do?"

Kate expected the usual surprise and banal comments, but Sharon seemed genuinely interested. In response to her questions, Kate grew animated, explaining the importance of her research.

"I'm hoping for a grant from the Cameron Foundation," she concluded. "They're very interested in the experiment I'm currently conducting."

"It must be wonderful to have a career." Sharon's eyes were shadowed with discontent. "I wish I'd prepared for one in college."

"You were a business major," Garrett reminded her.

"Big deal. Who would hire me?"

"I would," he said. "I've told you that before."

"Don't you think there are enough of us in the business already?"

"You can take my job," Trevor offered. "I'm sure you'd be equally good at it."

"I understand Sharon's reluctance," Kate said. "She wants to be hired on her own merits. But forget about the Carriage House being a family business," she advised the other woman. "I think you could be a real asset."

"I did enjoy working there during the holidays," Sharon admitted. "I didn't put in the time Garrett did, but I'm not totally without experience."

"Give it some thought," Kate urged. "You don't have to be stuck in a rut." She glanced at Garrett and added softly. "A very kind man taught me that. I owe him a great deal."

"I'm sure he's rewarded every time he looks at you," Garrett answered in a husky voice.

Chapter Six

The dance lasted quite late, but Kate was wide-awake on the drive home. She wanted to discuss every detail of the evening.

Garrett was touched by her excitement. "I'm glad you had a good time," he said gently.

"I can't believe I was dreading tonight. I'm so happy you made me go."

"I didn't *make* you go."

"Yes you did, Garrett, and you were right. I can't believe I have three dates next week!"

"Do you have a preference for any of the three?" he asked casually.

"I don't know them well enough yet. Ian is the smoothest, but Chris has a good sense of humor, and Mitch is such a nice person."

"So basically you're not attracted to one more than the others?" Garrett persisted.

"You mean physically?"

"Just out of curiosity."

Kate thought about it. She'd danced with all of them without feeling the shiver of excitement she always experienced in Garrett's arms. That must be the feeling he got when he danced with Lorna, Kate thought poignantly, remembering their absorption in each other.

Garrett was waiting for a response so she said lightly, "I guess I won't know until they kiss me."

He turned his head to frown at her. "I don't expect you to behave like a teenager."

Kate began to laugh. "You sound like a worried parent."

"You're half right, anyway," he muttered.

"I've missed out on a lot of experiences. You told me yourself I should be warmer with people."

Garrett stopped the car in front of her house and took her firmly by the arm. When they were inside the apartment he confronted her ominously.

"I want you to listen to me, Kate, because I feel responsible for you. You don't know how you affect men. The three you'll be dating are nothing like Palmer. They won't pressure you, but they're not going to back off if you start sending out the wrong signals. They could easily get the idea that you're interested in more than a few innocent kisses."

Kate was secretly thrilled by his vehemence. It meant he cared a little about her anyway. "You're telling me not to be promiscuous," she said demurely.

"Is *that* what you got out of it?"

"Yes. You don't want me to sleep around. I don't know why you're worried, though. You must know I wouldn't do that. At least not on the first date," she added mischievously.

"My God! What have I done?"

He was so obviously distressed that she took pity on him. "I was only teasing you because you're making a big deal out of nothing. If you ever get married and have a daughter, she's going to grow up thinking a kiss is one of the four-letter words."

"If you want to get kissed so badly, I'll be happy to oblige." He jerked her into his arms.

Garrett's mouth was angry at first, but it softened against hers. His lips moved in a sensuous invitation that was reinforced by his powerful body pinning her firmly. Kate's lips parted mindlessly for the male invasion of his tongue. Her arms slid around his neck as she responded totally, uttering a small cry of pleasure.

His fingers tangled in her long hair and one arm tightened around her waist, bonding her even closer. She could feel every taut muscle in his rigid body as she moved instinctively against him.

He released her abruptly. Gripping her shoulders to put her away, he glared down at her dreamy face.

"Now do you understand why I'm concerned?" he rasped. When she continued to gaze at him in mute invitation, unable to shake off his spell, Garrett swore under his breath. "Go to bed, Kate," he ordered, striding out the door.

She didn't follow his instructions immediately. The evening had been filled with revelations, but Garrett remained a mystery. Could he kiss her like that without feeling something? And if he did, why was he so determined not to get involved? Was he so committed to Lorna that no other woman stood a chance?

Kate was afraid that was the answer to all her questions. She was trying to find something that didn't exist. Garrett had kissed her twice. Once to restore her self-confidence, this time as an object lesson. He didn't know it was unnecessary. No other man could evoke such a response from her. The sad truth was, she'd fallen in love with Garrett.

Kate walked slowly to the full-length mirror and gazed at herself in the lovely gown that was supposed to make dreams come true. It hadn't quite lived up to its promise.

The telephone woke Kate the next morning.

"You sound sleepy," Garrett said. "Don't tell me you're still in bed on this glorious day."

A glance at the clock on the nightstand showed it was only nine o'clock. "We got to bed late last night," she answered defensively.

He chuckled richly. "That sounds a lot more provocative than what really happened."

Kate became fully awake. "Are you one of those terrible people who make jokes in the morning?"

"Don't tell me you wake up grumpy?" he countered.

"Only until I've had my coffee."

"Drink instant this morning. I want to make good on the rain check I gave you for a day at the beach."

"Why didn't you tell me last night?"

"What difference does it make? Do you have other plans?"

"No, I . . . I just like to know these things in advance."

"Be spontaneous," he advised. "I'll pick you up in an hour."

"I'm still in bed," she protested.

"What are you wearing?" he asked unexpectedly.

"A nightgown, naturally."

"Naturally," he repeated dryly. "Flannel, no doubt. Get dressed, Kate. I'll be over shortly." He hung up before she could respond.

Kate was indignant at Garrett's assumption that she slept in a granny gown. Actually she was wearing a peach-colored silk-and-lace nightgown.

As she raced around showering and getting dressed, Kate's resentment changed to speculation, then to cautious optimism. Why had Garrett asked what she was wearing? So he could picture her in bed? Maybe his devotion to Lorna wasn't complete, after all. That would certainly make it a new ball game.

Kate paused in front of her full-length mirror before putting on jeans and a T-shirt, trying to look at herself from a male point of view. Her breasts were small, yet high and firm, and her long legs were slender and well-shaped. Lorna's figure might be more voluptuous, but hers was every bit as good in its own way.

If Garrett didn't already know that, he was about to find out. Kate's mouth curved in a smile as she glanced at the pink bikini on the bed.

Garrett's beach house was furnished for comfort rather than show. One wall of the living room was completely lined with books, and reading lamps were positioned near couches and chairs.

The wall facing the ocean had sliding-glass doors that led onto a deck cantilevered over the sand. A flight of stairs led down to the beach.

"What a glorious view you have," Kate exclaimed, staring out at the blue Pacific.

"I find it very restful, but some people prefer the city view from my apartment. There isn't much to see here at night."

Kate surmised that "some people" meant Lorna. "I think it would be very romantic to walk along the sand in the moonlight," she commented artlessly.

"I'm told it messes up the hairdo," he said dryly. When Kate started to laugh, Garrett asked, "Did I say something funny?"

"I was thinking of that old joke: One way a man can tell a woman is crazy about him is if she'll make love right after having her hair done."

He looked at her with a raised eyebrow. "I never expected to hear anything risqué out of you."

"You're talking about the old me." Kate smiled enchantingly. "I'm a new woman."

"You're an accident on its way to happen," he answered darkly. "I can only hope your mother told you about the birds and the bees."

"I could never understand what that had to do with sex."

"I never could, either," he admitted with a slight smile. "But I assume she did tell you the facts of life."

Kate kept her expression bland. "I'm a scientist. I know all about how cells reproduce."

"Great. That's going to come in handy," he muttered.

"It's really fascinating. Would you like me to explain how spermatozoa reach the ova?"

"No!"

"I suppose it *would* take away some of the thrill of implantation," she remarked judiciously.

"Are you putting me on?" he asked with sudden suspicion.

Her suppressed laughter gave her away. It finally pealed out despite all her efforts.

"You little devil!" he exclaimed. "You've been giving me the impression that you intend to hop into bed with the first guy who asks you, just to see me react."

"It serves you right. You should know better."

"That's true. You couldn't change *that* much."

She slanted a glance at him. "I could if I really loved someone."

Garrett seemed to lose interest in the subject. He answered her almost indifferently, as he moved around the room replacing books from tables to the bookcase. "Just be sure you don't confuse love with infatuation."

"I'm scarcely an adolescent," she said in frustration.

"Then don't act like one." He picked up her canvas beach bag. "I'll show you where the guest room is. Shall we go for a swim before lunch?"

"I guess so." Kate followed him down the hall, slightly crestfallen. She evidently had a few things to learn about the art of seduction.

The guest room was small and it didn't face the water. It was comfortably but not sumptuously furnished with a double bed, a chest of drawers and two chairs. A door led to a bathroom with a tiled shower but no tub. A guest would be well provided for, yet not pampered.

This gave Kate a choice of two conclusions. Either Garrett didn't welcome guests, or his female ones weren't housed here. That was the more obvious answer.

"This room doesn't look as if it's used much," she commented innocently.

"Not a great deal. I like privacy when I come down here."

"Don't you get lonely?"

He repressed a smile. "It hasn't been a problem."

Because he wasn't alone. It was a sure bet that Lorna didn't use this room when Garrett brought her here.

"Come down to the beach when you're ready," he said, leaving her alone.

Kate's hopes were renewed after she'd changed into her bikini. It was blatantly sexy while remaining in good taste. A wide ruffle circled her hips and another edged the brief top, covering the tips of her breasts. The total effect was more titillating than revealing. She put on sunglasses and walked confidently to the door.

Garrett was already on the beach, standing with his back to the house and staring out at the ocean. The snug pair of white bathing trunks he was wearing contrasted vividly with his deep tan. Kate paused on the deck, seizing the opportunity to admire him openly without his knowledge.

His legs were slightly apart and his hands rested on his narrow hips. Motionless like that in the brilliant sunshine, he resembled a magnificent bronze statue of a perfectly proportioned Greek god.

Kate remained very still, but as though he could sense her presence, Garrett turned around. Untamed desire glittered in his eyes as his gaze traveled swiftly over her. The emotion was gone in an instant, however.

"Be careful on the stairs," he called. "One of them is a little rickety."

Kate wasn't disturbed by Garrett's casual greeting. She'd seen his reaction, fleeting though it was. Lorna was losing ground by the minute.

Garrett was an accomplished swimmer, but Kate was his equal. Only his superior strength allowed him to outdistance her. They frolicked in the water like a couple of porpoises, alternately diving under the waves and floating on top.

When they finally waded ashore Garrett said, "That was exhilarating. I'll take the ocean over a pool any day."

"I agree with you," Kate said.

As she stumbled on the sand, he put an arm around her waist to steady her. "You're one of the few women I've met who feel that way. Most prefer a pool."

"That's because they can keep their heads out of the water." Kate smiled up at him. "Other things are more important to me than a hairdo."

He removed his arm. "You can wash your hair later. There's a dryer in your bathroom."

He kept distance between them as they dried off, then stretched out on large beach towels spread on the sand.

When the sun was directly overhead, Garrett said, "I'm getting hungry. How about you? Do you like grilled hot dogs?"

"Love them."

"That's good. I don't know what I would have done if you'd said no." His white teeth gleamed in a grin. "Hot dogs and hamburgers make up my entire repertoire."

"How about chicken?"

"I tried it once. It turned out black on the outside, and raw when you cut into it."

"You probably had it too close to the coals. I'll show you how to do it next time—if I'm invited back."

"You're welcome any time," he answered politely, but vaguely. Standing up, he brushed sand from the golden hair on his muscular legs. "I'll start the fire in the barbecue."

Kate watched as he lit the coals, then trailed after him when he went inside to get the food.

"This is a marvelous kitchen," she commented, glancing around at all the modern appliances.

"I suppose so. I don't use it much," he answered, taking bottles and jars out of the refrigerator.

"That's a shame."

"I don't come down here to cook."

"I suppose not," she murmured.

He gave her a look of annoyance. "You're obviously picturing this place as a swinging bachelor pad, but you couldn't be further off the mark. As I said before, I come down here to unwind.''

"You don't have to explain to me," she answered neutrally.

"No, I don't." He thumped down a jar of mustard.

Attempting to control his irritation, he checked over the items on the kitchen table. Besides hot dogs and buns it held a bottle of catsup and jars of relish, pickles and olives.

"I think that does it, unless you want onions on your hot dog."

Kate shrugged. "Sure, why not? I don't have to worry about getting too close to anybody."

Garrett's eyes flashed blue fire. Jerking her into his arms he grated, "Since you're so determined to be kissed, we might as well get it over with."

This time his mouth didn't soften against hers. It was demanding, openly sexual. Kate tensed instinctively, but he didn't relax his steel grip. She was welded to his hard frame, bruised by the corded muscles that dug into her more delicate flesh.

The tiny whimper she uttered finally penetrated Garrett's fury. His punishing hold loosened, although he didn't release her. The probing exploration of her mouth became an invitation rather than a demand. His caressing hands moving over her bare skin heightened the seduction.

Kate was throbbingly aware of how closely their bodies were joined. A couple of scraps of fabric were the only barrier preventing them from experiencing each other fully. As Garrett trailed his fingers suggestively down her spine, flames spread through Kate's midsection and her legs began to tremble.

In a gesture that was becoming familiar, he suddenly moved her away, keeping his hands on her shoulders.

Looking at her dispassionately, he said, "I hope this will teach you not to play games."

After a shocked moment Kate turned and ran out of the kitchen to the guest room, needing to escape. How could Garrett be so calm after displaying such passion? How could he turn his emotions on and off, first hot, then cold?

Color flooded Kate's cheeks as she remembered her unbridled response, even after his initial brutal kiss. She should have at least *tried* to struggle, even if it wouldn't have accomplished anything.

The galling thing was that Garrett knew she wouldn't resist. He was teaching her another of his odious lessons. Anger began to simmer inside Kate. Maybe she'd provoked him a little, but Garrett had no right to humiliate her like that.

"Lunch is ready." His voice came through the closed door, sounding as normal as though the earth hadn't rocked briefly in its orbit.

"I don't want any," she answered tightly.

"I've already fixed you a hot dog. With onions." His voice held suppressed laughter.

That was the last straw! Kate marched to the door and flung it open. "You might think what happened in there was funny. I don't! You hurt me!"

"Only your feelings, and I'm afraid you deserved that."

"You're no gentleman," she stormed.

"I'm sorry for losing my temper, but that's all I regret. Taking advantage of your inexperience would have been contemptible."

"I didn't expect . . . I mean, I didn't want you to . . ."

"I know. But playing with fire can get out of hand," he said gravely.

"You've made your point." She turned her back and went to stare out of the window.

"In that case, let's have lunch."

She whirled around at the sheer incongruousness of the suggestion. "You expect me to sit down with you and eat a hot dog?"

"It's all I have." He smiled. "We could get in the car and go to the hamburger place up the road, if you'd rather."

"You know that's not what I meant."

"Are you going to let this little incident break up our friendship, Kate?"

"I wouldn't call it a friendship." She sighed, her anger draining away. "I can't decide *how* you feel about me."

"Very fondly," he answered gently. "You should know that by now."

It wasn't what Kate wanted, but she either had to settle for that or give up Garrett completely. That might be the wiser course since her love was returned only by affection, but Garrett had become an integral part of her life.

"Can't we forget about this?" he coaxed.

She summoned a smile to signal a truce. "It isn't something I care to remember."

"Then let's have lunch. I'm starving."

Kate couldn't help feeling self-conscious at first. She was the one who made sure not even their fingers touched. But Garrett was so completely natural that she eventually relaxed.

After lunch they took the Sunday newspaper down to the beach and lounged on a blanket under an umbrella anchored in the sand. The soothing murmur of the ocean made Kate drowsy after a while.

"Nobody would ever have to take a sleeping pill if he lived by the ocean," she yawned.

"It's very peaceful," he agreed.

"I'll bet all your problems disappear when you get into bed at night."

"Almost all of them," he said as he watched her long lashes flutter down.

Kate was awakened some time later by the sound of voices. Garrett's sister and brother-in-law were standing on the deck.

"We just dropped by for a minute," Sharon called when she saw Kate lying on the blanket. "We aren't staying."

As Garrett got up and strolled over to them, Trevor said apologetically, "I told Sharon we should have phoned first."

"No problem," Garrett assured him. "Kate and I were just lying around reading the paper. Put on your bathing suits and join us."

"You don't have to be polite." Trevor grinned. "We're family."

"If I didn't want you, you'd know it," Garrett joked. "Leave your things in the guest room with Kate's," he said casually.

Since he seemed sincere, Trevor and Sharon allowed themselves to be persuaded. While they were changing, Sharon looked thoughtfully at Kate's neatly folded clothes on the bed.

"I believe Garrett is finally serious about a woman," she proclaimed.

"Because he took Kate out twice in a row?" Trevor asked incredulously.

"No. Because her things are in here instead of Garrett's room."

"You think he's in love with her because he isn't sleeping with her? Even Garrett gets turned down sometimes."

"That's one possibility," Sharon conceded. "Although you can tell she's attracted to him."

"That doesn't mean she's going to hop right into bed. They've only known each other a short time." Trevor sat down to pull off his shoes and socks. "You're also forgetting about Lorna. Garrett's been involved with her for months."

"Involved is the right word," Sharon answered disgustedly. "He's been trying to get out of her clutches for a long time, but she hangs on like a leech. Kate would be much better for him."

"It's not your choice to make," Trevor responded with unaccustomed sharpness. "Do you have to run everyone's life?"

"Garrett isn't everyone, he's my brother." She looked at her husband with a slight frown. "What's the matter with you lately? You snap my head off over the slightest thing."

"I'm sorry." He ran a hand through his hair. "I haven't been sleeping well. I guess I'm a little edgy."

"Maybe you should go to the doctor for a checkup," she said with concern.

"Over a slight case of insomnia?" He forced a smile. "What kind of nut do you think you're married to?"

"I can answer that one." She framed his face in her palms and gazed at him lovingly. "The dearest man in the whole world."

He gathered her in his arms and buried his face in her hair. "I never want to hurt you, Sharon."

"You couldn't hurt anyone," she said tenderly. "I know I'm too bossy at times, but it's only because I love you and Garrett so much. I want him to have as good a marriage as we do."

Trevor released her. "I'm sure Garrett won't disappoint you."

The two couples spent a pleasant afternoon, alternately swimming and basking in the sun. It was late afternoon when Garrett suggested drinks. Trevor accompanied him into the house to help make them.

When they were alone on the beach Sharon said to Kate, "I hope we didn't spoil your day."

"No, I'm really glad you came," Kate answered.

Sharon laughed. "We must be more charming than I thought. Most women would prefer to spend the day alone with Garrett."

"Like Lorna?"

"You know about her?" Sharon asked cautiously.

"I met her at the country club last night. And I saw Garrett dancing with her. That told me all I needed to know," Kate said in a flat tone of voice.

"I'll bet you misinterpreted what you saw. She likes to give the impression that Garrett is crazy about her."

Remembering the look on his face last night and his actions today, Kate was forced to agree with Lorna. It was wishful thinking to believe otherwise.

"You don't have to reassure me," Kate said evenly. "My relationship with Garrett is strictly platonic."

After a look at her remote expression, Sharon changed the subject. "I've been considering what you said last night. Do you really think I should take Garrett up on his offer of a job?"

"Unless you feel you and Trevor would be spending too much time together. Problems can sometimes crop up when couples work at the same place and see each other constantly."

"It would be a welcome change. We don't see nearly enough of each other now. Trevor works late a lot of nights, and sometimes he even goes in on Saturday."

"You should tell your brother to stop being such a slave driver."

"Garrett is an even worse workaholic," Sharon exclaimed. "He really *should* go into politics. He'd certainly get things done."

"Is he considering it?" Kate asked curiously.

"I think it's a long-range plan. He's enjoying his term as foreman of the grand jury."

"I didn't know that either," Kate said slowly.

"What do you two casual acquaintances talk about?" Sharon teased.

Garrett appeared on the deck carrying a tray. "Come and get it," he called.

As they sat around sipping tall drinks, Sharon inspected the sparse contents of two small bowls. One held pretzels, the other salted peanuts.

"Don't you ever have anything to eat in this house, Garrett?" she asked.

"I'm not here very often," he answered.

"You could keep hors d'oeuvres in the freezer and some cans of smoked oysters and pâté in the cupboard. The Carriage House has an entire gourmet section. Why don't you visit it sometime, so your guests don't starve to death?"

"That's unjust. I grilled hot dogs for Kate today."

"That must have made this a day to remember," Sharon said disgustedly.

Kate's cheeks felt warm, as she said to Garrett hurriedly, "Sharon has been telling me a lot of things about you I never knew."

"I'm almost afraid to ask," he remarked dryly.

His sister gave him a reproving look. "I simply told her you were on the grand jury."

"How is that different from a regular jury?" Kate asked.

"We hear pretrial testimony on cases and then decide if the evidence warrants handing down an indictment."

"Don't you have to be a lawyer?"

"No. Our panel is made up largely of businessmen like myself."

"And you're the foreman. I'm impressed," Kate said.

"It's no big deal. All you need is an unblemished reputation." Garrett smiled. "They like to keep the good guys and the bad guys on opposite sides of the law."

"I don't know where you find time for all the things you do," Kate marveled.

"There is always time for the important things."

"Speaking of important things, how about dinner?" Trevor asked.

"You're right, we'd better get going." Sharon finished her drink and stood up.

"Don't rush off," Garrett said. "I plan to take everybody to the lobster place on the highway."

"Take Kate. Trevor and I are going to head for home," Sharon said as she and her husband went to change out of their bathing suits.

It had been a pleasant, relaxing afternoon, due in part to the presence of the other couple. Kate felt her nerves tensing at the prospect of being alone with Garrett again.

"I have to go home, too," she said hastily.

"Everybody's deserting me," he complained. "Are you sure you can't stay for dinner?"

"I couldn't go to a restaurant looking like this." She lifted a lock of her limp hair.

"You can wash it here."

"That would take so long, and tomorrow is a workday."

"I have an alternate idea. I'll go out and get some takeout food while you're showering and washing your hair."

Before she could answer, Sharon and Trevor came to say goodbye. "Thanks, Garrett, it was fun," Sharon said. "I'll call you next week, Kate. Maybe we can have lunch together."

After they'd left, Garrett asked, "What would you like me to get? Ribs? Chicken?" He took it for granted that Kate had agreed to stay.

"Whatever you like," she answered helplessly.

"Okay. I'll take a quick shower first. You can take your time."

Kate knew she'd given in to Garrett because she wanted to. The chance to spend the evening with him was more compelling than a few qualms. A ripple of anticipation traveled through her as she shampooed her hair.

Kate had just stepped out of the shower when the doorbell rang. She must have dawdled longer than she thought. Knotting a large towel around herself and wrapping another around her head, she ran to the door barefoot. Garrett had either forgotten his key or his hands were full.

She opened the door saying, "That was fast. I'm not—" The words died as she was confronted by Foster Gray and an exotic brunette.

"Well, hello again." His eyes made a comprehensive circuit over her. "We have to stop meeting like this."

Kate turned crimson, knowing the impression he was getting. "Garrett isn't here," she said breathlessly.

Foster's eyebrows climbed. "You're here alone?"

"No, I . . . he went out to get something."

"I see," he murmured. "We just stopped by for a drink, but perhaps this isn't a convenient time."

"You can wait if you like. I have to dry my hair." Kate fled back to the bedroom.

She knew it was stupid to care what Foster thought of her. She didn't even like the man. There was something unpleasant about him, a kind of smarminess. Anyone else might reserve judgment in a situation like this, but he was the sort of person who automatically assumed the worst.

Kate had just turned off the hair dryer when Garrett knocked at the door. "I'm back," he announced.

She opened the door and looked over his shoulder. "Is he still out there?" she whispered.

"Who?"

"Your friend Foster. He was here with some woman."

Garrett frowned. "That's what I get for mentioning that I planned to come down here today. Is he coming back?"

"I hope not. It was so embarrassing. I could tell he thought I'd spent the night."

"I'm sure you're imagining things."

"I don't like him, Garrett. He makes me feel . . . crawly."

"Come and have dinner," Garrett said soothingly. "It's all ready."

A table in a corner of the living room was illuminated by a squat candle. It cast a mellow glow over the appetizing food Garrett had dished out.

"This chicken should be good," he commented after they were seated. "The chef was just taking it off the barbecue."

"It's delicious," Kate said, although she was only picking at her food.

He watched her for a moment before saying gently, "You mustn't let Foster upset you."

"There's something about him. I honestly don't know how the two of you can be friends."

"Old loyalties die hard," Garrett answered slowly. "Foster and I were roommates in college. We did all the wild and wonderful things you're supposed to do before you grow up and accept responsibility. But Foster never made the transition. He's still a rebellious teenager looking for a way to beat the system."

"You're part of the establishment he holds in contempt. How do you know your loyalty is returned?"

"I might not approve of his life-style, but I have no reason to doubt his integrity." Garrett looked troubled as he added, "At least not toward me."

Kate realized she wasn't going to change Garrett's opinion. Nor did she have a right to try. The bond between the two men was their own business. She had a deep-rooted suspicion, however, that Foster wasn't worthy of Garrett's trust. By tacit agreement the subject was dropped.

The chicken was as delicious as Garrett had predicted, and cleaning up after dinner was a breeze. They threw out all the cardboard containers and put the dishes and silverware in the dishwasher.

"I always hate to leave here," Garrett commented as he blew out the candle in the living room.

"I don't blame you," Kate said. "It's too bad I didn't go back with Sharon and Trevor. You could have stayed the night."

"Your company was more than adequate compensation," he answered warmly.

"I'm flattered." As a small silence fell she said, "Well, I guess we should start back to town."

"It's early yet. Would you like to walk on the beach?"

"I've had my exercise for the day." She laughed. "I'd rather just look at it."

"An even better idea. I wouldn't mind relaxing for a few minutes." He piled pillows on the arm of one of a pair of long couches facing each other across a glass coffee table.

"What are you doing?" she asked warily.

"Fixing a place for you to lie down." He went to the other couch and did the same thing. "I often lie here at night and watch the ocean. It's a great tension reliever." He stretched out full-length with a contented sigh.

After a moment's hesitation, Kate followed his example. The couch was wide and deep, blissfully comfortable. Moonlight lit the room, and soft music came from the stereo.

"Isn't this great?" Garrett asked.

"Heavenly," she agreed.

They talked in a desultory fashion, punctuated by companionable silences.

The last thing Kate said was, "I knew it would be like this at night. The ocean is...so...soothing." Her eyes closed and she slept.

Garrett watched her for a long time, a tender expression softening the rugged planes of his face. Finally he regretfully called her name. When she didn't stir, he went to stand over her and try again. This time she stirred but didn't waken.

After a moment of indecision Garrett took an afghan from the back of the couch and draped it over her. Bending down, he touched his lips to hers with exquisite gentleness.

Kate smiled in her sleep and uttered a tiny sound of pleasure.

Chapter Seven

Kate was awakened at dawn the next morning. The sun was burning fiery patterns on her closed eyelids. She opened her eyes to see blue sky and sparkling water instead of her customary bedroom wall.

She wasn't in her own bed, either. For an instant she thought it was a dream. When she saw Garrett asleep on the other couch, Kate sprang to her feet.

Her inadvertent cry woke him. He opened his eyes and smiled at her. "Good morning. Did you sleep well?"

"Is that all you can say?" she demanded sharply.

His smile widened to a grin. "You said you didn't like jokes in the morning."

"This isn't a joke, it's an outrage! Why didn't you take me home last night?"

"You were already asleep, so it seemed pointless."

"It never occurred to you that I might not want to spend the night with you?" she asked acidly.

"I was a perfect gentleman. I didn't even undress you."

"At least you showed one grain of sense," she muttered.

"Also great restraint. Doesn't that prove I was merely being a good host?"

"I don't think this is funny, Garrett. Yesterday you showed your displeasure very graphically when you thought I was playing games. Now you're doing the same thing."

"I'm sorry, honey." His amusement fled. "I did try to wake you, but you were really zonked. I honestly didn't see any harm in letting you sleep. Nothing happened, and nobody was hurt by it."

Kate realized that Garrett was right. She'd jumped to all the wrong conclusions. "I'm sorry if I overreacted. I never spent the night with a man before. I guess I expected it to be different," she joked.

"Are you telling me—" he broke off abruptly. "I'll make coffee."

While the coffee was perking Kate used the new toothbrush Garrett gave her, and he dressed for work.

When he came into the kitchen, resplendent in a suit and tie, she smiled. "We don't make a very well-matched couple." She gestured at her own jeans and T-shirt.

"It would seem that way," he answered grimly.

Garrett was abstracted on the drive back to the city. He answered her comments mostly in monosyllables except when he said, "I'd offer to stop for breakfast, but I want to get to the office early."

"That's all right," she answered. "I have to get dressed and go to work too."

When he dropped her off at her apartment his leave-taking was brief. "Take care," was all he said.

* * *

Kate pondered the change in Garrett as she changed clothes. He was like a different person after she joked about never having spent the night with a man. Was that such a crime? What difference did it make to him, anyway? Garrett had made it clear that he had no designs on her. And now he certainly didn't.

Well that was just fine with her, Kate told herself angrily. She didn't need him anymore. There were plenty of attractive men in the world who considered it a privilege to be with her. If experience was all that mattered to Garrett, he was wise to stick to the voluptuous Lorna. They deserved each other.

Kate continued her silent diatribe all the way to work, sustaining her anger to ward off the hurt underneath.

When she reached the lab, Dwight was donning his white coat. He gazed admiringly at her golden tan. Since her rebellion the previous week, he'd begun to regard her as a person rather than a convenience.

"Did you go to the beach over the weekend?" he asked.

"Yes," she answered curtly, not wanting to talk about it.

Thinking she was still miffed at him, Dwight tried to make friendly conversation. "I envy you. My wife dragged me through the stores to look for baby furniture."

Kate realized he was trying to make amends, so she forced herself to unbend. "No sense in putting it off until the last minute."

"I guess so, but I kind of miss the carefree days when we did things spontaneously. The baby isn't even here yet, but it's already changed our lives."

"You're finding out what making a commitment means." Her soft mouth tightened. "Even mature men have trouble with that."

He slanted a comprehending glance at her grim expression. "Take my advice and don't be in too big a hurry to get involved. Big things are in store for you."

"Like what?"

"I heard a rumor that you're the front-runner for that science grant."

Her face cleared. "Where did you hear that?" she asked eagerly.

"I can't tell you. It's very hush-hush, but I got it on good authority that it's between you and one other person, and your project has a higher priority."

Kate's elation lasted through the day. Her work was always engrossing, and the hours flew by. Garrett and the events of the weekend were crowded out of her mind.

When she went home that night, however, he filled her thoughts again. She certainly had a knack for falling in love with the wrong men. Not that her hero-worship of Palmer had been love. The real thing was a lot more painful.

Kate knew everything was over between them, but she couldn't help hoping Garrett would phone. Just to say hello. After all, he was the one who told her he'd always be her friend. But he didn't call.

The evening seemed to drag on interminably. By the time she gave up waiting for the phone to ring it was too late to go to a movie, which is what she should have done earlier. Kate grimly promised herself that she'd never spend another night like this one. From now on, Garrett was history.

When the phone finally rang her resolution was forgotten as she raced to answer it.

Her aunt's voice greeted her. "You sound rushed. Did I get you away from something important?"

"Oh . . . hi, Aunt Jen. No, I was just watching television." Kate tried to cover her disappointment. "Is everything okay over there?" Kate asked.

"Just dandy, except for the bottles that blew up in the basement."

"You had an explosion?" Kate asked excitedly. "Are you all right?"

"It was nothing. I was making beer and I must have put in too much yeast."

"You don't even drink beer!" Kate exclaimed.

"I know, but other people do, and it's always good to be prepared," her aunt replied placidly. "A nice teller at the bank gave me the recipe."

"You can buy beer at any market. Why would you try to make it?"

"For the same reason people climb Mount Everest. I've never done it before."

"Nor again, I hope. You might have been hurt," Kate scolded.

"I could be kidnapped by aliens from outer space, too, but I can't sit around worrying about it."

"They wouldn't have to kidnap you. You'd be first in line for a boarding pass."

"Wouldn't I be foolish to turn down a free trip?"

Kate smiled unwillingly. "I'd like to think you're joking, but I wouldn't bet on it."

"You can't go through life being careful, Kate. Any experience is better than no experience."

"*Some* people agree to that theory."

The older woman was alerted by the bitterness in her niece's voice. "Well, enough about me. What have you been doing?" she asked casually.

"Oh, this and that."

"You were going to your high-school reunion the last time I spoke to you. How was it?"

"Has it been that long since I called you?" Kate asked remorsefully.

"Don't give it a thought. I'm not one of those demanding old ladies who whine about being neglected."

"It's the other way around," Kate answered fondly. "I'm delighted when you make time for me."

"Always for you, pet. Now tell me about the reunion. Is that young man you had a crush on still gorgeous?"

"I suppose a lot of women would think so."

"But you obviously don't. That's good. It shows you've matured."

"I'm not so sure." Kate's voice was somber. "I'm still a rotten judge of men."

Aunt Jen hid her interest under a light tone. "You mustn't get discouraged. Everyone makes a mistake now and then."

"How about two in one week?"

"With different men, I hope. I'd hate to think you failed to learn by experience."

"They were separate disasters, but that still makes me a chump."

"At least you seem to be having an active social life."

"If the next three dates are like the last two, I might go back on the inactive list."

"Where are you meeting all these men?" Aunt Jen asked. "I hope you're not going to one of those dating services. Call me old-fashioned, but I don't think you can find romance through a computer."

"They're probably more accurate than the emotional approach," Kate answered dully. "I have a bad habit of going off the deep end for every handsome hunk I meet.

At least a computer would toss out the ones who aren't interested.''

"I can't imagine any man being that dense," her aunt stated crisply. "They must have been cretins."

"One was, but the other wasn't." Kate was unaware of the poignancy in her voice.

"I see," Aunt Jen murmured. "Well, life is full of surprises. Perhaps the more appealing one will have an attack of common sense and realize what he's passing up."

"Maybe." Talking about Garrett, even indirectly, was too painful. Kate changed the subject. "Are you busy next Sunday? We could go somewhere for lunch and spend the day together."

"I was hoping you'd ask," Aunt Jen replied.

Kate left work right on time the next day, although she wasn't enthusiastic about her date with Ian that night. Still, it was better than spending another evening like the previous one.

He arrived on time, bearing a large bouquet of red and white roses. As he handed them to her he said, "The red rose whispers of passion and the white rose breathes of love. I thought I'd cover all bases."

Kate smiled. "It sounds as though you've been browsing through your *Bartlett's Quotations*."

"I was hoping you'd think I made up those lines just for you." He grinned. "Actually they were written by a nineteenth-century poet named John Boyle O'Reilly, but don't I deserve points for the time I spent looking for them?"

"Absolutely. The thought is what counts. Even if it wasn't your thought," she teased, taking the flowers into the kitchen to put them in water.

Ian followed her. "Lawyers aren't very poetic, unfortunately."

"I didn't know you were an attorney."

As soon as she'd made the comment, Kate braced herself for a stupid joke about showing her his briefs. Palmer wouldn't have passed up the opportunity. But Ian was a lot more polished than that.

"Formal attire covers a multitude of sins," he remarked. "Did I mention that you look smashing tonight?"

"Thank you. I didn't know where we were going, so I wasn't sure how to dress."

"I made reservations at the Crystal Palace. I hope that's all right."

"It's perfect," Kate answered. "I've been wanting to go there."

The Crystal Palace had recently opened in a former nightclub. Los Angeles was a city hungry for innovation, and the gimmick there was an ice rink instead of a dance floor. At intervals throughout the evening, diners were entertained by an ice show.

When they'd arrived and were seated at a choice table, he smiled meltingly at her. "Do you believe in fate?"

"Not that our whole lives are preordained. I think we have choices. If we make the right one we call it fate, but if we make the wrong one we chalk it up to bad luck." Kate's apathy had disappeared and she was beginning to enjoy herself. Ian was easy to be with, and his obvious admiration was balm to the pride Garrett had wounded. *Ian* didn't consider her unsophisticated. He was clearly overjoyed to have gotten a date with her.

"How can anyone so beautiful be such a cynic?" he chided. "Fate was responsible for our meeting. I almost didn't go to the dance Saturday night."

"I almost didn't either," she admitted, remembering how Garrett had practically forced her.

"See there?" Ian exclaimed. "It *was* predestined for us to meet."

"I also met Chris and Mitch the same night," she pointed out mischievously. "How do I know which of you fate was aiming me at?"

"They're no competition," he answered dismissively. "If the choice was between Garrett or me, I'd be worried."

Kate's smile faltered. "Garrett is involved with Lorna."

"He's been taking her out for months, but he's had long-term relationships with other women. None of them has ever lasted. That's why I was afraid you were his new interest."

"I can assure you I'm not," Kate answered bleakly.

"That's good. Garrett is dynamite with women."

"Don Juans don't interest me," she said coolly.

"I wouldn't exactly call him a Don Juan. That name is applied to the love 'em and leave 'em type, but Garrett isn't that kind of guy. He's pretty decent, really. I don't think he makes any promises he doesn't intend to keep."

"How about letting a woman think he cares, when he doesn't really?" Kate was dismayed to hear the bitterness in her voice, but Ian evidently didn't.

"Very often people believe what they want to believe. It's a sad fact of life that you can't *make* someone love you."

She certainly knew that to be true! How did you get over loving somebody who didn't want you, though?

"Hey, why am I pleading Garrett's case, when I want you to concentrate on me?" Ian asked.

"I have no idea." Kate mustered a smile. "You're the one I want to hear about. What kind of lawyer are you?"

"A good one, I hope," he joked.

"I'm sure of that. I meant what do you specialize in?"

"I'm a corporate attorney. My branch of the law doesn't lend itself much to anecdotes. Unless you want to hear how Wainwright versus Macabie set a precedent that changed the fiduciary liability of elected officers of a company."

"Will it affect my ability to get out of bed in the morning?"

"Only if you forget to set your alarm clock."

Ian's law practice wasn't as dull as he pretended. He told her fascinating things about the world of high finance and some of the flamboyant people involved. Although he deprecated his own importance, Kate got the impression that Ian was a very able attorney.

He also encouraged her to talk about her own career. She explained her work in detail because he really seemed interested. The intelligent questions he asked proved as much.

It was a thoroughly satisfactory evening. The food was good, the show was entertaining, but most of all, Ian's company was stimulating. Kate felt as though she'd made a good friend.

Not until he took her home did she realize she was being unrealistic. Ian wanted more from their relationship. At the door of her apartment he took her in his arms.

"I had a wonderful time tonight," he said in a husky voice. "I hope you did, too."

"Yes, I enjoyed it very much," she answered, her body tensing.

"I know this is our first date, but I was comfortable with you from the first moment."

"We did find a lot to talk about," she said tentatively.

"You're utterly fascinating, Kate. I've never been so instantly attracted to a woman."

As his head descended she forced herself not to flinch. Of course he would expect to kiss her, but this wasn't a repeat of that shabby incident with Palmer. Ian's hands didn't attempt to stray over her body. His eyes held desire, but not the unbridled lust Palmer had displayed.

Kate relaxed and lifted her face for his kiss. She genuinely liked Ian. Maybe he was the answer to her hopeless love for Garrett. It was self-destructive to continue yearning for the unattainable.

Ian was an experienced man. His lips moved over hers, enticing, coaxing. Kate tried to respond. She clasped her arms around his neck and let her mouth soften against his. But when his embrace tightened, molding their bodies, Kate stiffened.

The pressure of his arms eased and he lifted his head to gaze down at her with restrained passion. "You're so enchanting, Kate. You're enough to heat any man's blood."

"It's getting late," she murmured awkwardly.

"Don't worry, honey. I'm not going to get carried away. Just promise you'll give me some serious thought."

"I enjoy your company, Ian," she answered carefully. "But we really don't know each other very well."

He gave her a smile. "That's easily remedied. I'll tell you my life's story in installments—one every night for the next month. I've had a very eventful life."

"Be serious," Kate protested.

"Okay, maybe that's too pushy. I'll settle for three weeks and then we'll renegotiate."

Kate smiled, relieved that he wasn't going to pressure her. "How about giving me the condensed version in one night? Next week. Same time, same place."

"I'll accept your terms, but understand that you're dealing with an attorney. I plan to appeal my case."

"I'll look forward to hearing your arguments." She kissed his cheek. "Good night, Ian. I had a great time."

Kate's smile faded after he left and she started to get ready for bed. She *had* enjoyed herself, but not romantically. No nerve ends had quivered when their hands brushed. Ian's kiss hadn't left her breathless and tingling.

She tried to tell herself love didn't hit like an earthquake. It built slowly from a solid foundation. Her rationalization fell apart when she remembered the shock of awareness that had jolted her the first time she laid eyes on Garrett.

All right, so maybe Ian wasn't the solution. There were other men in the world. Mitch or Chris could be the one. As she turned out the light, Kate knew she was lying to herself.

The busy week Kate spent should have made up for the fact that Garrett didn't call. It didn't, however. Every time the phone rang she ran to answer it, tense with anticipation. But Garrett's curt farewell the previous Sunday was evidently final.

Kate's social life was successful in every other way. Ian sent flowers and phoned every night. Chris was similarly intrigued after their date on Thursday. He took her to the theater, one of Kate's favorite forms of entertainment. They talked for hours over supper afterward, and she found him excellent company. When he kissed her good-night as Ian had, she cooperated fully, but the result was the same.

Kate knew she should be grateful to Garrett. He was responsible for her newfound confidence and her active personal life. It seemed strange that he wasn't interested in how everything was turning out, considering all the time he'd invested in her. Could Garrett be waiting for her to phone with a progress report?

Kate weighed the pros and cons of that possibility for the remainder of the week. If Garrett didn't want to hear from her, it would be embarrassing. But if he did, she must seem terribly thankless.

On Saturday morning Kate stopped debating the point and dialed Garrett's apartment. Her heart was thumping rapidly as she waited to hear his voice, but a woman answered. For a moment Kate was speechless with misery. She wanted to hang up, but her reflexes weren't functioning.

"Hello," the woman repeated impatiently. "Who is this?"

"I, uh, I'm a friend of Garrett's. An acquaintance, actually. If you're ... if he's busy I can call back later." Kate was disgusted with herself for babbling, but she couldn't help it.

"He isn't here."

"Is this Lorna?" Even in the midst of her wretchedness Kate had to know.

"No, I'm the cleaning woman. Mr. Richmond is at his office."

A heavy weight lifted off Kate's chest. "Thank you," she said. "Thank you very much."

The traumatic experience discouraged her from calling Garrett at the store. But as she showered and dressed,

Kate thought of another item to add to her list of errands. She really needed some panty hose.

After picking up her cleaning, taking a pair of shoes to the shoemaker and a few other chores, Kate drove to the Carriage House. In addition to the panty hose she bought a new lipstick and looked at purses.

Finally Kate faced up to the fact that she was procrastinating. Either she went upstairs to see Garrett or she wrote him off as a lost cause. There wasn't much to recommend the second choice.

His secretary was pleasant yet businesslike. "Is Mr. Richmond expecting you?"

"No. I was in the store so I thought I'd drop by."

"He's rather busy this morning. We're having our semiannual clearance."

"Then I guess this isn't a very good time." Kate smiled weakly and turned to leave, convinced she was getting a strong message.

"Let me ask if he can see you," Sylvia said.

"I'd rather you didn't." Kate's protest was ineffectual as the other woman spoke into the intercom.

The door of Garrett's office opened almost immediately and he appeared in the entry. "Kate, how nice to see you. Come in."

"You're busy, Garrett. I don't want to disturb you."

"Nonsense. I'm delighted that you stopped in. What brings you here on a Saturday morning?"

"It's the only day I have to shop," she answered, following him reluctantly into his office.

"I'm pleased that you chose the Carriage House."

"Doesn't everyone?" she asked lightly.

"We like to think so."

That seemed to cover the subject. Kate's nerves quivered as she gazed at Garrett. He was fantastically handsome in a light gray suit and a blue shirt that matched the color of his eyes. But the conventional attire didn't prevent her from picturing the lithe body underneath. She'd experienced every hard contour, with very little between them to blunt the sensation.

Looking away hastily she said, "I won't stay. I'm sure you have things to do."

"No more than usual. Sit down for a minute." He waited till she perched stiffly on the couch, then took the chair facing her. His long body was completely relaxed, in contrast to hers. "How's everything going?"

"Just fine." Kate smiled brightly. "Actually, that was the reason for this visit. I wanted to thank you for introducing me to Ian and Chris."

"It sounds as if your dates were a success."

The disinterest in his voice stung Kate. Pride made her answer enthusiastically, "I had a marvelous time. They're both fascinating men."

"Do you have any preference?" Garrett asked casually.

"It would be hard to choose at this stage. I like both of them so much."

"There isn't any reason to choose. You need to meet a lot more men before you're experienced enough to decide."

"You make falling in love sound about as exciting as comparison shopping," she answered tartly.

"I didn't know we were talking about love."

"Men and women do experience the emotion. Although you probably find that hard to believe," she couldn't help adding.

"I believe it in your case. You have a habit of falling in love with very little provocation."

Kate was incensed. "At least *I'm* capable of caring for someone."

He looked at her impassively. "You think I'm not?"

Kate knew he was thinking of Lorna. Hopelessness engulfed her. Coming here today had been a gigantic mistake.

"How on earth did we get so serious?" she asked, rising. "All I came by for was to say thanks."

"It wasn't necessary, but I was happy to see you." He followed her to the door. "Which of the lucky two are you favoring tonight?"

"Neither. I have a date with Mitch."

"You'll like him. Mitch is very entertaining."

She wasn't thrilled by Garrett's seal of approval. "I'm looking forward to the evening." She was anxious to leave by now, but Garrett kept delaying her.

"Have any of them given you trouble?" he asked.

"No, they've been perfect gentleman."

"Unlike me." His firm mouth curved in a derisive smile.

Kate's heartbeat accelerated, but she kept her voice even. "You were never a threat. I realize that now."

"You're still underestimating your appeal, I see," he answered softly.

Anger gripped Kate. Garrett had demonstrated his lack of interest, but he couldn't resist tormenting her. Out of male vanity because she always reacted to him? Or did he guess her true feelings? The thought was chilling.

"You don't have to bolster my self-confidence any longer," she said tautly. "Other men are doing it for you."

"That pleases you, doesn't it?" He looked at her searchingly.

"Why wouldn't it? After all these years I'm getting the attention that women like Betty got in high school."

"Exactly," Garrett said in a flat tone of voice.

"Is that so terrible?" she asked defensively.

"No. It's entirely normal." He became suddenly preoccupied. "Have a good time tonight, and thanks for stopping by."

The visit to Garrett had accomplished one purpose, Kate reflected as she drove home. He'd made his feelings crystal clear. Anything that had existed between them, including friendship, was definitely over. She needn't wait by the telephone or manufacture reasons to see him. Garrett was out of her life forever.

He evidently neglected to share the news with his sister, however. Sharon phoned Kate a short time later. "I hoped I'd catch you in," she said. "I called a couple of times this week, but you were out."

"If you'd left a message I would have called you back."

"I hate those answering machines and it wasn't important, anyway. I just wanted to chat. It was fun at Garrett's last Sunday. Don't you simply adore that house?"

"Yes, it's very nice," Kate answered tepidly.

"I love lying in bed and watching the water at night."

"The guest room doesn't have an ocean view."

"Trevor and I borrow the house sometimes when Garrett isn't using it. We take his room. I do think he should drape the windows though, don't you? The sun wakes us up at an ungodly hour."

"I've never seen Garrett's bedroom," Kate said, to set the record straight.

"You're kidding! I didn't mean that the way it sounded," Sharon said hastily. "I merely assumed he'd shown you through the house."

"I saw all the parts I was interested in," Kate answered coolly.

"Poor Garrett. I guess he was bound to get shot down sometime, but I was hoping for a long-term relationship between you two. Oh well, it doesn't have to affect our friendship. Can you have lunch with me at the club today?"

Kate knew she should refuse. The prudent thing would be to sever all ties to Garrett, but she genuinely liked his sister. It had been a long time since she'd had a close woman friend.

"I can meet you in an hour," Kate said, making up her mind.

They had lunch on the terrace overlooking the pool, which was crowded. The tennis courts were also being fully utilized, and foursomes were strung out along the velvety green golf course.

"Is it always this busy here?" Kate asked.

"Only on the weekends, when the men aren't working. Except for my husband." Sharon sighed. "I don't know what I'm going to do with that man."

"Learn to live with it. Trevor isn't a sports nut. He's doing what he wants to do."

"I'm not so sure," Sharon answered slowly. "He's been so tense lately. I'm really worried about him."

"Has he been to the doctor for a checkup?"

"That's what I suggested, but he just shrugged it off."

"Do you think there's something he's not telling you?"

"I can't believe that. We've always told each other everything." Sharon smiled happily. "That's one of the wonderful things about marriage."

"I imagine it would be," Kate answered in a muted voice.

"I'm probably making a big deal out of nothing," Sharon said dismissively. "I'd just like to have him around more, like he used to be."

"The business world is demanding. Sometimes things pile up and you have to put in long hours to get them cleared away."

"I know. I'm acting like a spoiled child." Sharon ducked her head suddenly. "There's Lorna. I hope she doesn't see us."

Her hope was futile. Lorna headed straight for their table. She was wearing a very brief tennis dress and her long blond hair was tied back with a bright scarf. She managed to look both chic and sexy in the casual outfit.

"I phoned you three times this week," she greeted Sharon without preamble. "Don't you ever return calls?"

"Hi, Lorna. You know Kate Beaumont, don't you?" Sharon asked without answering the other woman's question.

"We've met," Lorna replied curtly.

"I thought you'd remember her." Sharon's expression was bland.

A flash of anger flared in Lorna's eyes. Ignoring Kate, she said to Sharon, "I wanted to ask what you're wearing to the Ransahoffs' party tonight."

Sharon shrugged. "It's informal, so I wouldn't get too dressed up."

"I asked Garrett, but he was no help." Lorna giggled, slanting a glance at Kate. "I won't tell you what he said he'd like me to wear."

"Thanks for not sharing that with us," Sharon replied.

"Garrett would have a fit if I did. He wouldn't want his little sister to know how naughty he can be." Lorna's voice was arch.

"You evidently see a side of him I don't. He was a perfect gentleman at the beach house Sunday, wasn't he, Kate?" Sharon asked.

Kate's color rose as she recalled Garrett's unrestrained behavior that day. The memory still made her bones melt. Lorna drew in her breath sharply, staring at Kate's flushed cheeks.

"By all means wear what Garrett wants you to, though," Sharon continued. "It might liven up the party."

"Thanks for the advice," Lorna answered acidly. She left without saying goodbye.

"That will teach her not to be overconfident," Sharon said with satisfaction as she watched the blond woman stalk away.

"Garrett won't thank you for trying to make trouble between them. Why did you?"

"Because I can't stand her. She was a pain in the ankle as far back as the first grade."

"You'll have to learn to like her if she becomes your sister-in-law," Kate said soberly.

"No danger of that. Garrett has been trying to break up with her for ages, but she always manages to wheedle him back. Lorna knows how to use every trick in the book on a man."

"She doesn't seem like his type—except for the obvious attractions," Kate admitted. "Garrett is so intelligent, though. I don't want to sound catty, but what do they talk about?"

"Lorna is no dummy. She had a good education and she has a sharp mind. Too bad she has the personality of a porcupine in heat."

Kate felt a sense of defeat. She and Sharon might not consider the other woman charming, but Garrett did. That was what mattered. Lorna would make him a perfect wife. They came from the same privileged background, they had friends and interests in common. What chance did an outsider have?

"Lorna is on her way out and I think she knows it," Sharon was saying. "That tacky allusion to her sex life with Garrett was meant to discourage you. She wants you to think they're making it night and day."

"He must have told her we're only friends."

"Garrett would never discuss one woman with another. Besides, you and my brother don't act like mere buddies."

"How do we act?" Kate asked warily. Had she given herself away in some manner?

"Like two people who are very much interested in each other."

"Would it change your mind to know Garrett made no effort to contact me all week?"

Sharon looked slightly crestfallen. "They've been awfully busy at the store. It's inventory time or something. Trevor's been putting in long hours, too."

Kate concentrated on pleating her napkin. "A man who's interested in a woman has time to make a phone call."

Sharon gazed thoughtfully at her bowed head. "You don't know Garrett when he's up to his elbows in work."

Kate forced a smile. "Well, it's nice that he's taking time off for relaxation tonight."

"I wish he'd asked you to the party," Sharon said unhappily.

"I couldn't have gone. I have a date with Mitch Davidson."

"I thought I saw Ian Colby trying to make time with you at the dance."

"I went out with him last Tuesday."

"Does Garrett know you're dating all his friends?" Sharon demanded.

"It was his idea. I really must run, Sharon. Thanks for the lunch. Next time it's on me."

Sharon couldn't understand what problem existed between Garrett and Kate. Their attraction to each other was obvious, yet both denied it. Why? That night at the party she was determined to find out.

The opportunity came during cocktails, when she found Garrett momentarily alone. "Come for a walk with me in the garden," she suggested. "I want to talk to you."

"That sounds ominous." He smiled. "What did I do now?"

"Nothing. That's the problem."

"Is there any way of pleasing women? You're damned if you do, and damned if you don't."

His amusement faded when they strolled outside and Sharon said, "What kind of game are you playing with Kate?"

"I don't know what you're talking about."

"Don't hand me that! First you monopolize all her time, then you drop her as if she gave you hives. That's rather unfeeling."

"You're making a big deal out of a few casual dates," he answered impatiently. "Kate isn't being neglected. She's seeing a lot of men."

"She told me it was your idea. Is that true?"

"Yes."

"Will you kindly tell me why you'd invite competition? Your testosterone level reaches the danger point every time you look at her."

"My hormones aren't your concern," he said austerely.

Sharon softened her approach. "I really like Kate, Garrett. You both seem so right for each other. I'm only trying to find out why you're acting so strangely toward her. I know she feels hurt. It isn't like you to lead a woman on just for kicks."

"You're talking about something you know nothing about," he said with restrained violence. "I'm doing what's best for Kate."

"Did Lorna make you choose between them?" Sharon asked suspiciously. "At lunch today she gave us the impression that you two rarely got out of bed. It's no wonder Kate was turned off."

His mouth thinned dangerously. "Exactly what did Lorna say?"

"I'd rather leave it to your imagination. Maybe she did you a favor," Sharon remarked innocently. "If Kate knows she doesn't have a chance with you, she'll be more receptive to someone who does care about her. Is that what you had in mind?"

He gave her a glare of annoyance. "Stop trying to manipulate me. If Kate and I are meant for each other, she'll find it out." Garrett strode across the grass and into the house.

Sharon watched his retreating back with a complacent expression. "*You* already know it, don't you, big brother?" she murmured.

Chapter Eight

Kate was drinking coffee and reading the newspaper on Sunday morning when the telephone rang. She'd long since given up hope of hearing from Garrett, so his voice came as a shock.

"I hope I didn't wake you this time," he said, as though they'd been in constant contact.

"No, I was just reading the paper," she managed to answer without stuttering.

"Have you looked out the window? It's a beautiful day."

"It's always beautiful in Los Angeles. A trained chimp could give the weather report if it could be taught to say, continued sunny, little change in temperature."

"True, but we're usually stuck indoors. Today is Sunday. We can go outside and play."

"Not together. We're on different teams." She wasn't going to let Garrett sucker her into having false hopes again.

"I thought I was your coach. Have you found someone to replace me?"

"I don't need anyone. I'm a different person now."

"*How* different?" he asked sharply. "You haven't done anything irresponsible, have you?"

"Like what?" She was honestly puzzled by his sudden harshness. Would she ever understand this man?

"Stop taunting me, Kate! Did you take my restraint as a rejection and decide to prove something to yourself?"

Comprehension suddenly dawned. Garrett thought she'd slept with one or more of the men she'd dated. That was bad enough, but it was his dog-in-the-manger attitude that infuriated her.

"If you're inquiring into my love life, it's none of your business," she said bluntly.

"The hell it isn't!" His anger surpassed hers. "Answer my question!"

"How would you like it if I asked what you and Lorna did last night?" she stormed.

"The truth would surprise you."

"I doubt it. I'm not easily shocked," she answered coldly.

Garrett's voice lost some of its heat. "Sharon told me about Lorna's regrettable performance at the club yesterday. I'm afraid she gave you the wrong impression."

"You don't have to explain anything to me. She wouldn't be *my* choice, but we obviously have different requirements," Kate said waspishly.

Humor crept into Garrett's voice for the first time. "Now who's inquiring into whose love life?"

"I couldn't be less interested," she answered loftily. "I hope you'll be very happy together. If you'll tell me when the wedding is, I'll send a present."

"That's very thoughtful of you, but Lorna and I won't be seeing each other anymore."

"Did you have an argument?" Kate asked curiously.

"Let's just say we agreed that our relationship wasn't going anywhere."

She couldn't imagine Lorna agreeing to that. Garrett was the one who had ended it. But why? Kate wanted to think she had something to do with his decision, but that seemed unlikely. A more logical explanation was that he'd simply gotten bored with the tedious blonde. No woman lasted forever with Garrett, Kate thought poignantly.

"I'm sure you'll find someone else," she said, suppressing a sigh.

"I'm not looking."

"You don't have to. She'll find you," Kate answered with a touch of bitterness.

"You're very good for my ego. How about coming to the beach with me today. That's why I called."

"I can't."

"It won't be a repeat of last week," he said quietly. "I promise not to touch you."

Did he think that was an incentive? Kate thought wryly. "I really can't," she repeated. "I'm having lunch with Aunt Jen."

"I guess I can't ask you to disappoint an old lady." Regret filled his voice.

Kate laughed. "You obviously have the wrong picture of my aunt. Her life is fuller than mine."

"She sounds more intriguing by the minute. I'd really like to meet her. Would she mind terribly if I crashed the party?"

"She'd be delighted. Aunt Jen adores male company. But are you sure that's what you want to do? She lives in Marina del Rey." Kate mentioned a suburb near the beach. "It would shoot your whole afternoon."

"I can't think of any way I'd rather spend the day. What time shall I pick you up?"

"If you're really serious, twelve o'clock will be fine."

Kate hung up feeling slightly dazed. How had she caved in so easily? Garrett bounced in and out of her life like an erratic tennis ball. He raised her hopes, only to dash them repeatedly. She ought to avoid him like the plague—except nothing could make her stop loving him. Therefore, any time with Garrett was better than no time.

As they drove down the freeway, Kate glanced around Garrett's gleaming Ferrari. "We should have taken my car."

"Because this is only a two-seater? Don't worry, I'll call a taxi to take us to lunch."

"That wasn't what I meant. Aunt Jen will find some reason to drive your car."

"It's a stick shift."

"That's the only kind there was when she learned to drive."

"Cars then didn't have the power they have now, though. She couldn't handle this one."

Kate grinned. "You want to bet?"

He slanted a suspicious look at her. "I have a feeling you're putting me on. You've built me up to expect an elderly hippie, and instead I'm going to find a sweet little old lady with Victorian manners and a cameo brooch on her bosom.''

"You're right on all counts.'' Kate's eyes brimmed with amusement.

"If she's so freewheeling, how did you grow up so inhibited?''

"It wasn't Aunt Jen's fault. She tried to make me more adventurous, but I guess my self-confidence was undermined by losing my parents at such an early age.''

Garrett reached over to squeeze her hand. "It didn't stop you from pursuing the career you wanted.''

"It's paying off," she agreed, her face lighting up. "That grant I told you about is coming nearer. I'm still almost afraid to hope they'll give it to a woman, but I was told I'm the front-runner.''

"Surely in this day and age they wouldn't discriminate on the basis of sex.''

"There's still a lot of it around. Men expect higher standards from women than they place on themselves. I'm as good a scientist as any of the men I'm in competition with, but the slightest hint of impropriety could tip the scales against me.''

"I can't imagine you doing anything improper," he said fondly.

"Not until I get my hands on that grant," she joked.

"Is your project top secret, or can you tell me about it?''

The miles flew by as they talked easily together. No sexual tensions were present, although Kate was keenly aware of Garrett's lithe body within touching distance of hers.

When they reached Marina del Rey she directed him to a quiet street with a few old houses tucked between modern apartment buildings. The old-fashioned homes were the last vestiges of a suburb that had experienced a population explosion of mostly young people.

Multi-unit apartment complexes with pools and saunas were inhabited largely by affluent singles. The marina was lined with their sail and power boats moored in front of an upscale shopping center. Numerous restaurants of every type were scattered among trendy boutiques. The young people strolling around on that Sunday wore brief shorts and even briefer tops.

Garrett had raised an eyebrow when they passed the place. "This is where your aunt lives?"

"She was here long before any of this was built."

"How does she feel about the changed character of the place?"

"Delighted. Aunt Jen thrives on young people." Kate pointed to a white frame house overshadowed by two apartment buildings. "We're here."

As they walked up the cement path, the front door opened and a tiny woman stood in the entry. Snow-white hair framed her pink-cheeked face. She was wearing a navy, calf-length dress with white lace collar and cuffs. A topaz brooch adorned her neckline.

"Dear child, it's so good to see you." She kissed Kate's cheek. "I'm also delighted that you brought your gentleman friend."

"This is Garrett Richmond, and he's only a friend," Kate said to prevent any misunderstandings.

"Isn't that what I said?" Aunt Jen's gray eyes were inspecting Garrett with lively interest.

"It's a pleasure to meet you." He extended his hand. "Kate has told me so much about you."

After letting her tiny hand be engulfed in his large one for a moment, Aunt Jen led the way into an old-fashioned parlor. It was cluttered with ancient furniture and knickknacks. Faded photographs in silver frames covered the mantel and numerous end tables, along with china figurines, small porcelain boxes and other bric-a-brac.

"Would you care for a glass of sherry before lunch? Or would you prefer something stronger?" Aunt Jen asked Garrett.

"Sherry will be fine," he answered. As he watched her pour the amber liquid from a crystal decanter into delicate glasses, Garrett remarked, "You're exactly the way I knew you'd be, in spite of Kate's attempts to mislead me."

The older woman looked at her niece with affection. "Kate doesn't have a devious bone in her body."

"Doesn't that make you ashamed of yourself?" Garrett asked Kate reprovingly.

Her eyes danced with mischief. "Garrett doesn't believe you're a motorcycle freak."

"Really, Kate. Your language skills are deteriorating. Besides, I realized that was impractical for a woman my age."

"I never thought you'd admit it," Kate said.

"I've always prided myself on being flexible. That's why I took up scuba diving instead."

Kate closed her eyes briefly. "Please tell me you're joking."

"It's quite safe. Too safe," her aunt sniffed. "The classes are held in a swimming pool. Isn't that ridiculous with an ocean a few steps away?"

Garrett turned to Kate with a slightly dazed look. "I owe you an apology."

"I could never invent Aunt Jen," she answered with a rueful smile. "Shall we go to lunch?" Kate asked her aunt.

"I'll get my purse."

After the older woman had left the room Garrett said, "I'm having trouble putting the two images of your aunt together. If she's really as modern as she seems, why does she live in the past?" His sweeping arm indicated the cluttered room.

"All these things have happy memories for her."

"Given her advanced ideas, I would think she'd prefer an apartment in a high-rise with contemporary furniture and all the latest gadgets."

"Aunt Jen enjoys the best of both worlds. She has the graciousness of bygone days, and adventure right outside her door."

As the subject of their discussion returned, Garrett stood. "Will it take long to get a taxi?" he asked. "Unfortunately my car only seats two."

Aunt Jen glanced outside at the red Ferrari parked at the curb. "Is that magnificent machine yours?"

Kate started to laugh. "Yes, but you can't drive it."

Her aunt ignored her, looking appealingly at Garrett. "I've never driven a sports car. Would you mind terribly? You and Kate can take my car and I'll meet you at the restaurant."

"I don't see what harm it could do," he said to Kate.

"Splendid," Aunt Jen said swiftly before her niece could intervene. She held her hand out for the keys. "How fast will it go?"

"Don't you know how to say no?" Kate demanded as the red car zoomed away from the curb.

He gave her a melting smile. "You Beaumont girls are irresistible."

Even though Kate and Garrett left the house later than Aunt Jen, they had to wait fifteen minutes for her in the restaurant parking lot. She arrived finally with ruffled white curls and a beaming smile on her face.

"Did you take a detour through downtown Los Angeles?" Kate asked pointedly.

"Don't be silly, pet. I merely went for a little spin up the highway. This automobile is exhilarating. I'd like to own one."

"Do you have any idea of how much they cost?"

After Kate told her, Aunt Jen's eyes widened. She gave Garrett a speculative look. "That's an enormous amount to pay for an auto."

"It's an expensive toy," he agreed. "I guess all men are boys at heart when it comes to their cars."

Kate's pulse quickened as she gazed at his smiling face. With a lock of wind-ruffled hair falling across his tanned forehead, Garrett was heart-stoppingly handsome. No woman would ever mistake him for a boy.

Aunt Jen was a silent observer. She looked thoughtful as she accompanied them inside.

Conversation flowed easily during lunch. They talked about a variety of subjects, but Aunt Jen managed to find out a great deal about Garrett without asking impolite questions.

While they were waiting for dessert Kate discovered a coffee stain on her sleeve. She excused herself to go to the powder room and put cold water on it. Garrett stood politely, then watched as she walked away.

"I looked forward to meeting you," Aunt Jen said when he sat down. "You're the first man my niece ever brought here."

He smiled engagingly. "Do I pass muster?"

"You're very nice-looking and you have excellent manners."

"Somehow I sense a but in there someplace," he said wryly.

Aunt Jen chose her words carefully. "Kate is a very unusual girl for this day and age. She has remarkable strength in some areas, but she's totally unsophisticated in others."

"That's obvious, but I would never take advantage of the fact," Garrett said quietly.

His statement didn't reassure the older woman. "Things were easier in my day." She sighed. "We didn't go from one person to another. When two people fell in love, they got married and settled down. I was married to my husband for thirty years."

"Didn't you ever feel as though you missed something?" Garrett asked intently.

"Like what?"

"The stimulation of going out with a lot of men. The admiration. The excitement of falling in and out of love."

"You're speaking of adolescence. I loved only one man in my adult life. The Beaumont women are like that." She glanced up and smiled. "Here she is now. Did you get the spot out?"

"Pretty much." Kate sat down and looked at the dessert, which had arrived while she was gone. "Doesn't this chocolate mousse look divine?"

Garrett agreed absentmindedly. He was uncharacteristically quiet during the rest of the meal.

After lunch they browsed through the shops, and Garrett insisted on buying Aunt Jen a pair of antique garnet earrings.

"Are you sure that's proper?" Kate teased. "I thought a lady only accepted flowers and candy from a gentleman."

"My intentions are honorable." His remark seemed to be directed to Aunt Jen rather than Kate.

"I'm so glad to hear that." The white-haired lady stood on tiptoes to kiss his cheek.

"I should have known better than to introduce you to a fascinating older woman," Kate complained.

"I only wish I were young enough to compete for him," Aunt Jen said with a twinkle in her eyes.

"You'd never know if she was after you or your Ferrari," Kate advised Garrett.

"Then I'd better stick to you," he answered, putting his arm around her shoulders.

It was almost five o'clock when Kate and Garrett arrived back at her apartment. The day had been so perfect that she hated to see it end.

"Would you like to come in for a drink?" she asked as he cut the motor.

"That would be nice." He followed her into the apartment.

Garrett lounged against the kitchen door, watching while Kate got ice from the freezer. His thoughts seemed to be elsewhere, though.

"Aunt Jen liked you," Kate commented.

"She's a remarkable lady. She gave me something to think about."

"I'd be surprised if she hadn't."

"Do you remember her husband?"

"Only vaguely. He died quite young. I just remember he gave me piggyback rides and he was very jolly."

"He's been gone a long time. It's surprising that such a vibrant woman never remarried."

"She's had lots of chances, but Uncle Henry was the love of her life."

"Do you really believe there's only one man for one woman?"

"In some cases. Aunt Jen is living proof."

"But what if sometimes it's only infatuation? Like the way you felt about Palmer, for instance." Garrett's voice was elaborately casual.

"That was a leftover from my teen years," she protested. "I wouldn't make the same mistake now."

He looked at her searchingly. "Are you sure?"

Sudden anger flashed through Kate. When was Garrett going to stop acting like a big brother? Several times that day she'd felt he was beginning to see her as a desirable woman, but that was self-delusion. He was once again delivering a lecture on playing the field before she made up her mind. Well, if that was what he wanted, that was what he'd get.

"You don't have to worry about me," she said with a tight smile. "I'm having too much fun to get involved with any one man."

Her anger registered. "I'm sure you've gained a lot of sophistication," he said gently.

The phone rang before she could answer. "Excuse me," she said curtly.

Chris's voice greeted Kate, giving her the perfect opportunity to get back at Garrett. She was a great deal warmer than she would normally have been.

"I didn't think I'd be lucky enough to find you in," he said.

She laughed merrily. "Then why did you call?"

"I can't stop thinking about you. Are you free tonight?"

"No, I'm afraid I'm busy." In spite of her momentary irritation with Garrett, Kate harbored a secret hope that he would suggest spending the evening together.

"How about tomorrow night?" Chris asked.

"I have a date then, too. But I'm looking forward to seeing you on Thursday," she said in a soft voice.

After consoling him for another few moments, Kate hung up with satisfaction. That would show Garrett that other men found her attractive.

He was standing when she returned. "I have to be running along. I enjoyed meeting your aunt. Thanks for a nice day."

"Oh." She looked for something more in his eyes, but found only impersonal friendliness. Suppressing her disappointment she said, "I'm the one who should thank you for the lovely lunch. Aunt Jen will write you a note."

Garrett's smile was spontaneous. "I'm sure she will."

Well at least he likes my family, Kate thought dispiritedly.

After he left she wondered if she'd overdone it on the phone just then. Garrett didn't seem angry or even annoyed, but any man's ego would suffer a little if he heard the woman he was with gushing over another man.

She'd done it only to give Garrett a tiny push. He'd been almost affectionate on several occasions that day. But if he *had* been starting to view her in a different light, the act she'd put on with Chris ruined all that. Garrett must think she was as giddy as a boy-crazy teenager. Kate sighed deeply. No matter what she did with Garrett, it was wrong.

In spite of her unhappiness over the situation with Garrett, Kate's days and nights were crammed with activity. She dated several times a week and often had lunch with Sharon. Garrett's sister had decided against taking a job at the Carriage House, and had gone back to college to get her M.B.A. instead.

"This way I can qualify for a position on my own," she explained to Kate over lunch one day. "I just wasn't comfortable with the idea of being handed a job because I'm Garrett's little sister."

"I can understand that," Kate answered.

"I'm eternally grateful to you, though. I never would have had the initiative to change my life if you hadn't lit a fire under me."

"I was only returning a favor." Kate smiled. "Garrett did as much for me."

"Do you see much of him?" Sharon asked casually.

"He's *your* brother. Don't you talk to each other?" Kate joked.

"Garrett doesn't welcome questions about his personal life. I only know he isn't seeing Lorna anymore. I was hoping it was because of you."

Kate pushed a bit of salad around her plate. "You're wrong. Garrett calls me occasionally, but it's all very platonic."

"You do see him though, don't you?" Sharon persisted.

"He takes me out once in a while. When he's at loose ends I suspect, so don't start imagining a big romance."

"I don't know what that man is looking for," Sharon grumbled.

"That's the point you're missing. He isn't looking. He told me so himself."

"I wonder what he's waiting for."

Kate tried to smile. "Maybe you and Trevor have set him an impossible example."

"That's very funny."

Kate's face sobered at her friend's expression. "Is anything wrong, Sharon?"

"I think so, but I honestly don't know what. Trevor has changed so much lately."

"In what way?"

"We don't communicate anymore. He comes home too tired to talk to me, but he's always willing to go out. It's almost as if he doesn't want to be alone with me."

"I'm sure you're wrong," Kate protested.

"Am I?" Sharon ducked her head and stared at her plate. "We rarely even make love anymore," she said in a low voice. "I'm beginning to wonder if there's someone else."

"You're letting your imagination run wild." Trevor wasn't the sort of man who would cheat on his wife. "It sounds to me as though he's wrestling with some problem. Could anything be wrong at work?"

Sharon smiled faintly. "Are you suggesting that he's juggling the books?"

"Of course not! I simply wondered if he was having difficulties with anyone in the office. Some of the people under him might resent the fact that he's an in-law."

"Trevor gets along with people better than I do."

"Under ordinary circumstances, but prejudice is hard to overcome. Have you spoken to Garrett about this?"

"No, and I don't intend to. Trevor would never forgive me. I shouldn't have told you either, but I'm so worried."

"It's probably nothing more than overwork," Kate said reassuringly. "Why don't you two take a vacation? A week in Hawaii would give you both a new perspective."

"You could be right." Sharon looked a little more cheerful. "I'll try to get him to go right after his birthday. That was another thing I wanted to talk to you about. I'm having a birthday party for Trevor a week from Saturday. I'd like you to come with Garrett."

"I'd love to come, but he might want to take someone else."

"It's my party, and I want him to bring you," Sharon said stubbornly.

"When are you going to give up?" Kate asked helplessly.

"It isn't a family trait."

"I'll be there under one condition. That you let Garrett make his own choice," Kate insisted.

Kate was sure Sharon had ignored her instructions when Garrett phoned that night.

"Did Sharon browbeat you into calling me?" she demanded.

"What gave you that impression?" he asked.

"I had lunch with her today. She asked me to Trevor's party and said she was going to tell you to bring me. I told her not to."

"You'd prefer to go with someone else?"

"No! I just don't want you to feel obligated."

"I'm a big boy," he answered dryly. "Trevor might have trouble handling my sister, but she doesn't intimidate me."

"Has Trevor talked to you?"

"About what?"

"I thought maybe he told you..." Kate hesitated, unwilling to violate a confidence. "Never mind. It isn't important."

"Does Trevor have a problem? Where did you see him?"

"I haven't. You were the one who said Sharon ran his life. I thought perhaps he'd complained to you."

"We stay out of each other's affairs," Garrett said. "That's why we get along so well. But don't write Trevor off as a wimp. I'm sure he takes a stand on the important things."

Kate wondered, even as she murmured an agreement.

"About the party," Garrett prompted. "Do we have a date?"

"I'd like very much to go with you," she accepted happily.

Although Kate had become friendly with Sharon, she'd never been to her home. When Garrett stopped the car in front of a stately brick house on the afternoon of the party, Kate's eyes widened.

"I had no idea they lived in a mansion," she exclaimed.

"It's large but not ostentatious," Garrett answered dismissively.

He was correct. Kate had been dazzled by Betty's house, but she soon recognized the difference between old and new money. Everything about the Hamilton home was quietly luxurious, from the mellow paneling in the library to the oriental rugs on the parquet floors and the extensive art collection on the walls.

The spacious rooms were cluttered with guests, and more people were congregated on the terrace at the back of the house. Waiters passed through the throng with glasses of champagne on a tray, but there was also a bar set up under a tented area on the lawn. After wandering through the house, Kate and Garrett eventually located Sharon in the living room.

"The country club might as well have closed down today," Garrett remarked, glancing around at the crowd.

"I omitted a few people." Sharon laughed.

"Who? The parking attendants? Atlanta didn't have this many bodies when they filmed *Gone with the Wind*."

"Don't be so grumpy. I know men hate cocktail parties," she confided to Kate, "but it's the easiest way to handle this many guests."

"Did you have to hold it on a Sunday afternoon?" he grumbled.

"I want to celebrate Trevor's birthday alone with him tonight," Sharon said softly.

"Don't you have any romance in your soul?" Kate scolded Garrett.

His eyes lingered on her lovely face. "I have plenty of it, but it isn't doing me much good."

A waiter paused to offer champagne. Kate accepted a glass, but Garrett refused.

"If you'll excuse me for a minute, I'm going to get a real drink," he said.

After he left, Sharon said, "I'd better warn you that Lorna is here today. We've been friends for so long that I almost had to invite her. I hoped she'd have the good sense to refuse, but no such luck."

"Was her breakup with Garrett traumatic?" Kate asked curiously.

"It was for Lorna. She's never given up anything willingly. I just hope she doesn't pick today to try and get him back."

"While he's with someone else? That's hardly likely."

"Don't underestimate her," Sharon advised. "She won't pass up any opportunity."

When someone came over to speak to Sharon, Kate went outside to find Garrett. She met Trevor on the way and stopped to say happy birthday.

"I don't know why everyone considers it a happy occasion." He smiled wryly. "What's so great about getting a year older?"

"You don't have to worry about that. You're in the prime of life."

"You mean this is as good as it gets?" His laughter held a false note.

Kate took a good look at him, noticing the lines of strain in his face. Sharon wasn't imagining things. Something was definitely bothering Trevor.

"Your grounds are beautiful," Kate remarked. That seemed like a safe subject. "I've never seen a real gazebo before." An octagonal-shaped summerhouse was visible in the distance.

"It's probably the only quiet spot here today. I'll show you the inside if you like."

As they strolled across the lawn Kate joked, "I hope you know I contributed to all this opulence. My bill at the Carriage House was astronomical."

"We like customers like you," he said lightly.

"I certainly couldn't afford to work there. I'd never get out of the store with my salary. You're lucky. Men are immune to temptation."

"Is that what you think?"

"Don't tell me you're a secret shopper?" she teased. "Is that why you spend so much time at the store?"

He paused at the entrance to the gazebo. "Has my wife been talking to you?"

Kate was taken aback by his hard expression. This was a side of Trevor she'd never seen before. "Sharon told me how dedicated you are to your job," she faltered.

"Why not? It's an important job." His mouth curved sardonically. "A lot of people would love to be treasurer of the Carriage House chain."

But not you, Kate thought silently. She was beginning to get an inkling of the trouble. "Sharon said you used to be the creative director of an ad agency," she remarked artlessly. "What exactly did you do?"

"It's a completely different world. You deal with words and ideas."

"Who were some of your clients? Would I be familiar with any of the campaigns you launched?"

"Unless you've been living in a cave in the Tibetan mountains." He named a list of famous products his agency had promoted. Trevor's face became animated as he recalled incidents from the past. "We had one client, a diet-foods manufacturer, whose wife insisted on being in the commercial. It was supposed to show two women with gorgeous figures tossing a beach ball around. His wife was a good twenty pounds overweight, but he wanted us to be the ones who turned her down."

"What did you do?"

Trevor chuckled. "We hired his girlfriend to be the other woman. When he realized they might start to compare notes, he was forced to do his own dirty work."

Kate watched as Trevor paced around the summerhouse, charged with energy. "You miss the advertising business, don't you?" she asked quietly.

His enthusiasm died like a match being blown out. "That's all in the past."

"Have you ever thought of starting your own agency?" Kate persisted.

"And break with tradition?" he asked mockingly. "The Carriage House is a family-owned business, and I'm family." His courteous mask slipped back into place. "Have you seen enough? I guess I should get back to the party since I'm the host."

"Go ahead. I'll be along in a few minutes," she answered absently.

Now that she knew the problem, Kate didn't know what to do about it. Trevor was the one who should tell his wife how he felt, not an outsider. But he clearly wasn't going to, and they were drifting dangerously apart. Maybe she should tell Garrett what she'd discovered. He might consider her presumptuous, though. She wasn't exactly an old family friend. Kate walked slowly back to the party, undecided about what to do, if anything.

Garrett met her on the lawn. "Where did you disappear to?" he asked. "I've been looking all over for you."

"Trevor was showing me the gazebo."

"If it was any other man I'd suspect hanky-panky." Garrett laughed. "But not with my brother-in-law."

"You're sure you really know Trevor?"

Garrett raised one eyebrow. "Don't tell me he made a pass at you. I'd find that hard to believe."

"No, of course he didn't! I was just wondering if you two ever sat down and talked."

He frowned. "This is the second time you've dropped hints about Trevor. Are you trying to tell me something?"

Garrett's frown was intimidating. "What could I possibly know that you don't?" Before he could answer, Kate said quickly, "Will you get me another glass of champagne? I put mine down somewhere."

Garrett was distracted, as she'd meant him to be. He took her hand. "Come with me. I don't want to lose you again."

While they were sipping their drinks a waitress stopped with a tray of hors d'oeuvres. Kate took a large shrimp and dipped it in cocktail sauce.

"Mmm, these are divine," she mumbled.

Garrett tipped her chin up and looked at her critically. "You have cocktail sauce on your mouth." When she licked her lips ineffectually, he said, "Let me do it." He dabbed the corner of her mouth with a cocktail napkin.

"Am I all right now?"

"You're perfect." He replaced the napkin with his forefinger and slowly traced the curve of her lower lip.

Garrett's feathery touch was making her tingle all over. "Nobody's perfect," she said with a shaky laugh.

"Whoever told you that was lying." His head descended a fraction toward hers.

She gazed up at him in a trance, waiting for him to take her in his arms. The people around them ceased to exist. Only Garrett remained, charging her body with urgency. Kate's lips parted unconsciously.

Garrett's sharply indrawn breath brought her to her senses. Why did his slightest touch always make her lose control? Kate glanced away in mortification—straight into Foster Gray's eyes. He was leaning against a tree, watching them.

When he realized his presence was noted, he sauntered over. "Quite a bash, isn't it?" Foster commented genially. "Your sister doesn't do things halfway."

"You know Sharon. How's everything going, Foster?" Garrett asked. "I haven't seen you around lately."

"Things are looking up. I'm sorry I missed you at the beach house that Sunday."

"You should have stuck around. Although Kate and I went home right after dinner," Garrett added casually.

"It's nice to see you two hitting it off so well together." Foster's smile included both of them. "I feel like a matchmaker."

"I'm afraid you're jumping the gun," Garrett answered evenly. "Kate and I are just friends."

"I did bring you together, though," Foster reminded him.

Before Garrett could answer, Lorna joined their group. She kissed Garrett's cheek and nodded indifferently to the other two. "Isn't it a marvelous party?" Her animated question was directed to Garrett.

"The gang's all here," Foster answered for him, glancing ironically from Lorna to Kate.

"You must be feeling a bit left out since you don't know any of Sharon and Trevor's friends," Lorna said to Kate.

"I know Garrett," Kate answered sweetly. "He's been wonderful to me."

Lorna's smug expression changed to anger. "Enjoy it while it lasts," she snapped.

Kate gave her an innocent look. "That's good advice for anyone."

Garrett didn't share Foster's amusement at the situation. "It's been nice seeing you both, but Kate and I have to leave."

"So soon?" Kate pouted. "I'm having such fun."

He took her by the wrist and strode away with a set face.

"I'm sorry if I upset your girlfriend, but she started it." Kate was breathless as she tried to keep up with his long strides.

"Now I know why men become monks," he muttered.

Kate's eyes glinted with laughter. "You wouldn't look good in a dress. Besides, I'll bet you secretly love having women fight over you."

"Oh, sure! I haven't had so much fun since my last root canal."

"Okay, I'm sorry. The next time I meet Lorna I'll tell her we only spent the night together once. Will that satisfy you?"

"Do me a favor." The corners of his mouth twitched. "Don't help me."

Chapter Nine

After they left the party Garrett asked Kate where she wanted to go for dinner.

"Are you hungry? Sharon had so much food."

"I like to sit down when I eat. Besides, I want something I can cut with a knife and fork. How about Windsor Court? Does that appeal to you?" It was a very expensive restaurant.

"That sounds elegant. I hope you have your credit cards with you."

Garrett patted his breast pocket reflexively. As he was about to reassure her, a surprised look dawned on his face. "It's a good thing you mentioned it. I forgot my card case. We'll have to stop by my apartment for a moment."

"I'll finally get to see where you live," Kate commented.

"I didn't know you wanted to."

"You mentioned the view several times."

"I was just going to run upstairs and come right down, but I suppose we can have a quick drink before we go to dinner."

Garrett had the penthouse of a tall building at the very top of a hill. Every room commanded a spectacular view of the city, and most of the rooms opened onto a terrace that wrapped around the entire apartment.

The furnishings were more formal than at the beach house, but the large couches and chairs looked comfortable. A wall of windows opened up the room to the outdoors.

Thick beige carpeting muffled Kate's footsteps as she walked over to look out while Garrett switched on some lamps. The view was indeed magnificent. Diamond-bright lights glittered in the darkness, some constant, some blinking on and off. Patterns formed and changed as cars darted about like shooting stars. The entire city was an incredibly beautiful kaleidoscope of mammoth proportions.

"When you said you had a view, I never envisioned anything like this," she marveled.

Garrett opened the sliding-glass doors so they could go onto the terrace. "Do you like it better than the beach house?"

"The two places are so different you can't compare them." Her dazzled gaze swept the magic scene. "You really have it all."

"Do I?" he murmured, staring at the pure line of her profile.

She turned her head to glance at him. "I can't imagine what more you could possibly want."

"You're right, of course." His expression was impersonal as he said, "I don't have any champagne on ice. Would you care for wine instead?"

"I've had enough to drink. Can we just sit here for a while?"

"Whatever you like."

"You're a perfect host." Kate smiled.

"I try to be."

"Do you have much company here? It's such a perfect place to entertain. You could accommodate quite a crowd."

"Sharon is the party animal in the family. I prefer small groups. The smaller the better."

Like one special woman, Kate thought. Lorna must have sat here many nights with him, enjoying the panorama. Perhaps they even had breakfast here the next morning. Kate got up abruptly to dispel the unpleasant image.

A sharp, ripping sound accompanied her action. A jagged edge on the metal chair had caught in her chiffon skirt and made a long tear all the way down the back.

Kate looked over her shoulder at the damage. "Oh, dear! I really did a number on myself."

"It wasn't your fault. I'll replace your dress, naturally."

"That isn't necessary," she protested. "It was an accident."

"I'm still responsible," he answered firmly.

"We can thrash that out later. What concerns me now is how I can go out to dinner like this." She examined the long split. "Maybe it won't show once I sew it up. If you'll give me a needle and thread, I'll do a quick repair job."

"That presents a bit of a problem," he said wryly.

"Don't tell me you don't have a sewing kit? What happens if you lose a button?"

"The laundry sews it on. You see, I *don't* have everything." He smiled.

Kate thought for a moment. "How about those little packets hotels provide?"

"You're a genius! I should have a couple of those. I don't know what I expected to do with them, but I seem to remember tucking at least one in my luggage."

She followed him as he went to find it. While Garrett took a suitcase from the top shelf of a closet, Kate glanced around his bedroom.

The room was large enough for a couch and an ebony wood table with two matching chairs, in addition to a king-size brass bed. The dark gray bedspread and tailored draperies were elegant yet unmistakably masculine. Colorful paintings on the white walls and a collection of framed photos scattered about, saved the room from feeling austere.

"I found it." Garrett returned holding a small cardboard folder that looked like a matchbook. Inside were a couple of needles and a small quantity of thread. "Will this do?"

"It's perfect," she said after inspecting the small packet.

He walked over to the table and switched on a lamp. "You can sit here by the light."

She looked at him doubtfully. "I'll have to take off my dress first."

"No problem. I'll wait for you in the living room."

Kate didn't know how to tell him she had on only panty hose under her dress. The gown had an attached slip and she hadn't worn a bra because the straps would have showed through the sheer fabric above the lined top. She'd feel uncomfortable sitting there almost nude.

"Could I borrow a robe?" she asked hesitantly.

"Certainly. I should have offered you one."

She went into the bathroom to change into the white silk kimono-style dressing gown he brought her. It was much too big, naturally. Besides that, the sleeves were too wide to roll up, and when she bloused the robe over the belt to keep from tripping, the front gaped open. Finally she returned to the bedroom, lifting the hem off the floor with both hands.

Garrett smiled when he saw her. "You look lost in that thing. Would you rather have a pajama top? At least you could roll up the sleeves."

"No, thanks. This will do fine."

The subtle male scent of him on the robe was disconcerting enough. Wearing Garrett's pajamas would be even more intimate. Kate concentrated on threading the needle so she wouldn't have to look at him.

"Do you need anything else?" he asked.

"A pair of scissors, if you have one."

"I do have *some* of the necessities of life." He chuckled.

"You have a lot more than that. I hope you appreciate all your blessings."

"This is the second time tonight you've reminded me," he answered dryly.

"It bears repeating." She glanced up at him curiously. "I wonder what it's like to know you can have anything you want. Does it take the edge off the pleasure when you get it?"

"I assume you're talking about material things."

"Those are what the average person wants."

"How about love?"

Kate's eyes returned to her sewing. "You can't buy love."

"Exactly. So I don't have everything," he said lightly.

"I'm sure you do. You simply haven't found anyone you want to accept it from."

He gazed at her bowed head. The lamplight had tipped her hair with gold. "Is that what you think?"

"Isn't it obvious?"

"What if you're jumping to conclusions?" he countered. "Suppose I fell in love with someone I couldn't have, for one reason or another."

"I'd suspect you were manufacturing obstacles because you didn't really want her."

"How can you say that without knowing the circumstances?" he asked sharply.

"I don't have to. Think about it," she advised.

He stared moodily at her. After a short silence he said, "That's taking a long time. Are you sure you can repair the damage, or would you rather go home and change?"

"That seems like a lot of bother. I'm almost through and I don't think the rip will show in the folds."

As she held up the skirt to demonstrate, the needle slipped out of the soft fabric and fell to the floor. Kate bent over to pick it up, but the needle eluded her in the thick shag carpeting.

"Damn," she muttered. "Where is the blasted thing?"

"Isn't there another one in the package?"

"Yes, but if I don't find this one you could step on it in your bare feet." She knelt on the rug and leaned forward, scanning the surface. "Help me look for it."

When Garrett didn't move, Kate glanced up to repeat the request. His almost graven pose told her something was wrong. Only then did she realize the front of her robe was gaping open. Garrett's avid gaze was riveted on her bare breasts.

With a gasp, she clutched the two sides together, her cheeks flaming. In her haste to stand up, Kate's feet tangled in the voluminous folds of fabric encumbering her. Thrown off balance, she flung out her arms to steady herself, and the robe parted once more. Garrett was kneeling in front of her before she could close it again.

Kate was mesmerized by the raw desire blazing in his eyes. She remained motionless, feeling her own tide of passion rising. She ached to have him touch her, to feel his mouth take deep possession of hers. Would Garrett deny them both yet another time?

She started to breathe again when he reached out, almost in slow motion. His fingertips touched her breasts so lightly that she might not have felt it if her skin hadn't been so sensitized. Then his palm cupped the swelling fullness of one breast and his thumb rotated savoringly over the stiffened nipple.

"Do you know how long I've wanted to touch you like this?" he asked huskily.

"I thought you never would," she whispered.

"Oh, Lord! I didn't want this to happen." He withdrew his hand reluctantly.

"*Why*, Garrett? What's wrong with me?"

He reached for her convulsively. "My darling Kate. How can you even ask such a thing? You're absolutely perfect."

"Then don't push me away again," she pleaded.

"I can't. God knows I've tried, but I can't."

His mouth closed over hers in a kiss so passionate that Kate's breath was sucked away. Once Garrett's defenses were breached, he was like a man possessed.

After untying the robe, he pushed it off her shoulders. When it slipped to the floor he caressed her feverishly, trailing paths of fire over her entire body.

"I knew you'd be this beautiful," he said in a hoarse voice. "I want to touch every exquisite inch of you."

He lifted her in his arms, carried her over to the bed and sat down, cradling her on his lap. While he parted her lips for an arousing kiss, his hand stroked her silken thigh. The caress, veiled by her panty hose, was more erotic somehow. Kate was uncertain whether the heat she felt was coming from his hand or her own body.

"I didn't know I could feel like this," she murmured.

"I do make you happy, don't I, sweetheart?"

"Happier than I ever thought I could be." She sighed.

He kissed her closed eyelids tenderly, then strung a line of kisses down her throat. Kate gasped as his warm mouth closed around her nipple. Tangling her fingers in his thick hair, she pressed closely against him.

"I want you so, Garrett," she moaned softly.

"I know, darling."

He placed her gently on the bed and stood up. Without taking his eyes off her, he undressed swiftly. Kate was fascinated by his broad shoulders and lean torso, but she turned her head away when he stripped off his shorts.

He gently urged her face back. "Don't be shy with me, angel. I want you to know me as intimately as I'm going to know you."

She forced herself to look at him while he knelt over her and slipped his fingers inside the elastic of her panty hose. Garrett's body was a flawless example of masculinity at its peak. She couldn't take her eyes off him, awed by the extent of his power.

Kate began to tremble when she lay completely nude and Garrett leaned down to kiss the soft skin of her inner thigh. She was gripped by feverish anticipation that kept mounting almost unbearably.

"I'll be very gentle," he soothed, misunderstanding the tremors that shook her.

She gazed up at him with deep emotion. "I love you, Garrett."

His face lit with exultation as he clasped her in his arms. The feeling of his nude body against hers was inexpressible. Kate arched her hips and strained against him to convey her urgency.

With a muted cry, Garrett parted her legs and completed their union. Kate stiffened in his arms, but he held her tenderly.

"Let it happen, sweetheart." He kissed her and stroked her breast.

She clung to him as he rekindled the fire. Gradually the flames spread and pleasure pulsed through her body. She moved tentatively at first, then with growing demand as waves of sensation drove her toward ultimate ecstasy.

She reached the peak, crying out Garrett's name in a kind of wonder. He shuddered with his own release then, holding her tightly. They lay quietly in each other's arms afterward, completely fulfilled.

Garrett stirred first. Smoothing the damp hair off her forehead, he looked at her searchingly. "Are you all right?"

She gave him a blissful smile. "I'm not sure. It must be illegal to feel this good."

His concerned expression faded. "Was it everything you expected?"

"You're wonderful," she answered softly.

"No, *you* are." He kissed her temple.

"You were very patient." She gave a tiny laugh. "I hope my enthusiasm made up for my lack of experience."

"I'll take enthusiasm any day," he answered with a smile.

"Did I really satisfy you, Garrett?" she asked hesitantly.

"In every way," he answered deeply.

"Why didn't you want to make love to me?"

His expression changed. "I've wanted you since the first night we went out together."

"But you fought against it. Why?"

"Because I don't believe in sex for its own sake," he replied curtly. "There has to be something more."

"I see."

Kate felt as though someone had thrown cold water in her face. What they'd just shared meant nothing to Garrett. He felt only lust for her. It should have eased the pain to know he desired her enough to forget his scruples. But it didn't.

She sat up, preparing to get out of bed. "I guess we both made a mistake tonight."

He caught her arm, preventing her from leaving. "I'm truly sorry, Kate. I promised myself I wouldn't take advantage of your inexperience. Can you ever forgive me?"

"It wasn't your fault. I wanted you as much as you wanted me."

"You only wanted to unravel the mystery of sex," he said sadly. "I just happened to be the man you chose to initiate you."

She stared at him incredulously. "Is that what you think? Don't you have any idea how I feel?"

He sighed. "Unfortunately I do."

"I *love* you, Garrett!"

"That's a common reaction. A first experience is a very emotional thing."

"What does it take to convince you? You know I was a virgin. I've never wanted any other man till I met you. Doesn't that tell you something?"

"Your experience with men was limited until I came along and changed your life." His mouth twisted. "That's what I get for trying to play God."

"Falling in love with *you* changed my life," she insisted.

"I wish I could believe that, but all the evidence tells me I'm wrong. Your whole face lights up when someone calls you for a date. Admit it, Kate."

She stared at him with dawning excitement. "You didn't really want me to go? You urged me to go out with other men because you thought that's what I wanted?"

"I know it is and I understand. You deserve all the flattery and attention you missed out on."

She slanted a glance at him. "How about sex? Do I have your blessing there, too?"

He hooked an arm around her waist and jerked her against his hard body. "I think I'd maim any man who laid a finger on you."

"Are you in love with me, Garrett?" she asked directly.

"I'm so crazy about you I can't think straight," he muttered. "I'm trying to do the right thing, but I want to be with you every minute of the day and night."

"I have a simple solution to your problem." She smiled enchantingly. "Let's get married."

"No. At least not yet."

"Sometime in the near future?" she coaxed.

Garrett hesitated. "Why don't we just leave things as they are for now?"

"You mean we both continue to date other people?" she demanded in disbelief.

"Just you." He cupped her cheek in his palm and gazed at her tenderly. "Marriage is forever, sweetheart. I've already found the person I want to spend my life with. I want to be sure you have, too."

Garrett's concern for her happiness brought a lump to Kate's throat. She hoped it wouldn't take long to convince him that he was the only man she'd ever love.

Sliding her toes up and down his calf, she said provocatively, "I suppose making love to me again could be considered undue influence."

He chuckled wickedly. "I'm not bucking for sainthood." His laughter died as he gazed into her eyes. "Darling Kate. You're the love of my life."

Tears of joy sprang to her eyes as she clasped her arms around his neck.

Their lovemaking was more leisurely this time. Garrett demonstrated all his expertise, exploring every erogenous zone of her body and encouraging Kate to become familiar with his.

Her shy efforts were tentative at first, but Garrett's response encouraged her. She experienced a sense of power when he groaned with delight at her intimate caresses. She became so adept that he pulled her down on top of him and locked his legs around hers.

"Are you trying to make me lose all control?" he demanded.

"Yes. I want to drive you crazy with desire." Her long hair tickled his chest as she slowly inserted the tip of her tongue between his lips.

"You've just succeeded, lady!"

Garrett rolled over with her in his arms. Smoldering passion glittered in his eyes as he poised above her for a charged moment before filling her with rapture. Kate rose and fell with the storm, until the final waves diminished into ripples of sated satisfaction.

Much later Garrett broke the silence. "We never had dinner."

Kate started to laugh. "Somehow I expected a more romantic declaration."

"Okay. Sweet Kate, I love you madly." He kissed the tip of her nose. "Now let's get something to eat."

"What time is it?" After glancing at the bedside clock she exclaimed at the lateness of the hour.

"We'll find a restaurant that's still open," he assured her.

"I have a better idea. I'll make something here."

"I don't know what there is," he said doubtfully. "I don't eat at home much."

"Well, let's go see what we can find."

As she started to put on his robe again, Garrett stopped her. "You'll break your neck in that thing. I'll give you one of my T-shirts instead."

The shirt was a lot more comfortable. The hem came to mid-thigh on her, and the short sleeves left her hands free. "This is a lot better," she agreed.

He looked her over with a gleam in his eyes. "I never knew my T-shirts could look so sexy."

"If you don't stop getting these primal urges it will be breakfast time before you get anything to eat," she teased.

"That gives me another idea. Will you stay the night?"

"I thought you'd never ask." She smiled.

He linked his arms around her shoulders. "You'll be lucky if I let you go in the morning."

"Maybe you won't have to," she said thoughtfully. "Could you take the day off tomorrow?"

"Don't you have to work?"

"I haven't had a day off in six months, not even when I had a miserable cold. They owe me," she said crisply. "If you can manage it, we could have such fun."

"What did you have in mind?" he murmured.

"We'll do that, too." She laughed.

"No man in his right mind would refuse an offer like that. The Carriage House can get along without me. Tomorrow I'm all yours."

"I'm gaining ground," she said mischievously.

The contents of Garrett's refrigerator weren't promising. Except for staples such as butter and eggs and bacon, Kate found only a bottle of white wine, some fresh fruit and half a roast chicken. She brought it out for closer observation.

"How old is this bird?"

Garrett looked at it warily. "I don't remember ever seeing it before. Maybe he flew in there and died."

"On one wing? It's only half a chicken."

"Then he deserves a decent burial."

"I'm inclined to agree with you."

After disposing of the chicken, Kate inspected the freezer with better results. It was filled with casseroles, neatly labeled with the contents.

"You've been holding out on me," she said. "Does some nubile maiden come in to cook for you?"

"Mrs. Krausmeyer would be flattered. She's about fifty and built along the lines of a lady wrestler."

"A likely story. Is there a Mr. Krausmeyer?"

"Either that or she has a boyfriend my size. If I don't wear one of my suits for a couple of weeks, she suggests I donate it to her favorite charity. Which I suspect is Mr. Krausmeyer."

"She has good taste in clothes, let's see how she can cook."

Kate put a beef ragout in the microwave. While it was heating she set the kitchen table and Garrett opened the wine.

"Where do you keep the wineglasses?" she asked, after failing to find them where the dishes were stored.

"In that cabinet next to the sink."

Assorted water and juice glasses were on the first two shelves, but the stemware was higher up. Kate stood on tiptoes, but she still couldn't reach them.

"Can you give me a hand?" she called over her shoulder.

Garrett came up behind her and cupped both hands around her exposed bottom.

"That wasn't the kind of hand I meant." She laughed.

"You'll have to more explicit." His palms glided over her hips to the top of her thighs. "I was just following orders."

"I don't recall telling you to do what you're doing now."

"This is my own idea."

Kate leaned back against him as his delicate exploration sent her pulse rate rocketing. "Is this how you keep the kitchen help happy?"

"Only when they wear my T-shirts with nothing under them."

"I hope Mrs. Krausmeyer never finds that out," Kate murmured when Garrett's hands moved up to her breasts.

The microwave-oven bell rang as Garrett turned her in his arms. Brushing his lips over hers, he said, "Don't you think it's too late to eat dinner?"

"Much too late," she answered.

* * *

Kate awoke in Garrett's arms the next morning, proving the night hadn't been a dream. When she mentioned her fear to him, his eyes darkened in a familiar way.

"Shall I prove I'm real?" he murmured.

"You're insatiable," she laughed, throwing back the covers.

"I seem to remember getting enthusiastic cooperation."

"A good houseguest is obligated to participate in the entertainment her host planned," she answered demurely.

"You were a very satisfactory houseguest." He chuckled. "I must remember to invite you back some time."

"You'll be lucky if I accept," she exclaimed indignantly.

"I'd be devastated if you didn't." He pulled her into his arms and gazed deeply into her eyes. "I don't ever want to lose you, Kate."

"You won't," she promised softly.

He kissed her then, with tenderness rather than passion. They whispered reassuring words of love to each other, but when Garrett's affection showed unmistakable signs of deepening, Kate drew back.

"We can't spend our whole lives in bed," she scolded.

"Why not?"

"Because sooner or later we'd starve to death. I'm going to make breakfast."

Kate cooked bacon and eggs, and made stacks of buttered toast with orange marmalade. They were both ravenous after having skipped dinner.

"What would you like to do today?" Garrett asked as he sipped his second cup of coffee.

"Well, let's see. It's a glorious day to be outside. Do you want to go to the beach?"

"I feel like doing something different."

"We could go to the zoo," she suggested. "I'll bet you haven't been there lately."

"Not in years. That's a great idea. I hear they have a fantastic reptile house."

"Ugh." Kate made a face. "I'll skip that, if you don't mind. I prefer things that have legs."

"You must be crazy about spiders."

"You know what I mean. I'll visit the lions and tigers while you look at your creepy crawlies."

They stopped at Kate's apartment first, where she changed into jeans and a checked shirt. Then they drove through Griffith Park to the zoo on top of a hill.

It was a lovely relaxing day. They strolled along the winding paths, holding hands and stopping to admire the magnificent wildlife. There weren't many people around on that Monday afternoon. The park was filled mostly with animal sounds and the twittering of birds until a group of small, boisterous schoolchildren appeared. Kate and Garrett watched in amusement as a couple of teachers and some harried mothers tried to keep the class from straying off in all directions.

"I don't envy them." Garrett grinned.

"Don't you like children?" she asked.

"I love them. Preferably in smaller numbers, though."

"Have you ever thought about being a father?"

His expression became impassive. "It's crossed my mind."

Probably in terms of avoiding the possibility, Kate thought. Garrett led her in the opposite direction from the children. His set face told her he didn't want to pursue the subject, but she couldn't let it drop.

"I'd like to have a baby, Garrett," she said quietly.

"What about your career?"

"A lot of women handle both."

"I doubt if it's as easy as the magazine articles proclaim. You have this idealized vision of life," he said impatiently.

"At least I'm not afraid to live it."

He put his hands on her rigid shoulders. "Don't rush things, Kate," he said gently. "For both our sakes, take time to be sure of what you want."

She was sure now, but perhaps Garrett wasn't. What if he'd felt this way about someone before and it hadn't lasted? Maybe his concern wasn't solely on her behalf. The thought of losing him was chilling.

"We're so happy now. Can't we just enjoy it?" he coaxed.

Since she couldn't force Garrett to marry her, Kate agreed, but the seeds of doubt had been sown. At first she was alert for signs of uncertainty on his part, but as the afternoon slipped away her suspicions seemed unworthy. Garrett treated her like the center of his universe. By the time they returned to her apartment, Kate was convinced she'd been borrowing trouble.

While she turned on the stereo, Garrett went into the kitchen to make drinks. "There's a message on your answering machine," he called.

She joined him in the kitchen. "It's probably only someone trying to sell me something. Everyone else knows I'm not usually home from work this early."

"It could have been there since yesterday. You weren't home last night."

"That's right. I forgot."

He raised one eyebrow. "I hoped I'd made a more lasting impression."

"What's that saying? Pride goeth before a fall." She laughed, turning on the answering machine.

Ian's voice was on the tape. "Sorry I missed you, love. I'll try again." After another beep he left a second message. "You're hard to reach, but I'll keep trying." On the third call he sounded plaintive. "What happened to you? Did you elope? Go away for the weekend? I hope you haven't forgotten our date Tuesday night."

Garrett had continued to fill the ice bucket without indicating any displeasure. "He's persistent, if nothing else," he commented casually after she'd turned off the machine.

"Ian has a lot more than persistence to recommend him," she answered, just as casually. Garrett couldn't have it both ways. He wanted her to date other men while assuring him they were wimps.

"Do you find him attractive?"

"You mean his personality or appearance?"

"Both."

"I'm not crazy about mustaches," she said consideringly. "But he's very charming."

"He seems to echo your feelings. Except about mustaches, of course." Garrett forced a smile.

She pulled a strand of hair over her upper lip. "You think he'd like me in a mustache?"

He cradled her face between his palms. "I think you could drive any man wild."

"That's good." She gazed at him provocatively. "What woman would want a tame man?" Kate closed her eyes in anticipation of Garrett's kiss, but he slung her over his shoulder instead. "What are you doing?" she gasped.

"You requested a caveman, if I interpreted correctly." He carried her down the hall to the bedroom. "Your wish is my command."

"Shouldn't you drag me by the hair?" she asked as he placed her on the bed.

His expression was infinitely tender as he bent over her. "Don't you know by now I could never hurt you?"

They made love with a passion that was more thrilling each time. He taught her new and stirring ways to give pleasure, delighting in her fulfillment as much as his own. After sharing the ultimate experience between a man and a woman, lying in Garrett's arms was a special joy.

When the telephone rang, it was an intrusion into their private world. "Let it ring," they murmured in unison.

The answering machine clicked on after the second ring and Sharon's voice came on. "I have to talk to you, Kate. Call me as soon as you come home, no matter how late it is."

Garrett and Kate looked at each other with concern. His sister's voice was high and strained. Before she finished the message, Kate picked up the bedside phone.

"I'm here, Sharon," she said.

"Oh, thank God!"

"What's the matter? You sound terrible."

"I need to talk to you right away. Can I come over?"

"How soon?" Kate glanced at Garrett.

"This minute! If I don't talk to somebody I'll go out of my mind. What little I have left."

"Of course you can come, but you sound so upset. Would you rather I came over there?"

"No! I have to get out of this house."

"Can't you tell me what's wrong?" Kate pleaded.

"Not over the phone. I'll be there as fast as I can."

Garrett got up and started to dress, staring at Kate with a worried frown. "What the devil do you suppose happened?"

"I don't know, but she's in a terrible state."

"Do you think I should stay?" he asked.

"She would have phoned you if there was anything you could do."

"That's what I don't understand. Sharon knows she can count on me if she's in some kind of trouble. We've always been close."

"I believe she wants to talk to another woman." Kate pulled on her jeans. "Don't worry. I'll call and tell you if it's anything serious."

They walked to the front door together. Garrett paused and hooked his hand around her nape. "I hate to leave you so abruptly."

"I know. But it would have been an early evening anyway. Tomorrow it's back to the salt mines for both of us." She smiled.

"It was a rare day." He lowered his head to kiss her. When their lips parted reluctantly he said, "I miss you already."

"I'll phone you," she promised.

"It won't be the same as having you there."

Kate didn't think this was the time to remind him that the situation could easily be remedied.

Chapter Ten

Sharon looked even worse than she'd sounded on the phone. Her face was drawn and she had deep circles under her eyes.

"Sit down and tell me what's bothering you," Kate said. "I've been imagining all kinds of things."

"Nothing like this, I'll bet. I've been such a fool!"

"Just take it easy," Kate said gently. "Would you like some coffee?"

"No...yes...oh, I don't know. I don't know anything anymore."

"Come in the kitchen with me."

While Kate made coffee, Sharon moved jerkily around the room. "I can't believe I didn't see what was going on. You think you know a person, but you don't really."

"It's Trevor, isn't it?" Kate asked quietly.

"He's having an affair with another woman."

That startled Kate. It wasn't what she expected to hear. "Are you sure?"

"Would I be such a basket case if I weren't?" Sharon demanded. "My marriage is over."

"Try to calm down and tell me about it."

"Remember the times I complained to you about how hard Trevor worked? How he didn't come home for dinner lots of nights and even went in on Saturdays? It seems I was worried about the wrong thing. Trevor was putting in overtime all right—with his secretary, Rachel Roberts."

"I can't believe that!" Kate exclaimed. "Not Trevor."

"That's what I would have thought. Not sweet, steady Trevor, the ideal husband," Sharon answered bitterly.

"You must be mistaken," Kate insisted. "What makes you think he's having an affair?"

"I was worried about him yesterday at the birthday party. He seemed tense and restless, but I didn't really get a chance to talk to him with all the people around. I thought we could sort out whatever was bothering him when we were alone that evening. I'd planned a romantic candlelit dinner at home for just the two of us."

Kate nodded, remembering that Sharon had mentioned it. "Did some of the guests stay on and spoil things?"

"They might as well have." Sharon stared down at her twisting fingers. "Let's just say things didn't work out as planned."

"I'm sorry," Kate murmured. "But sometimes that happens."

"More often than not lately," Sharon answered somberly. "I asked Trevor if anything was wrong, and he said he was just tired. I pleaded with him to stay home today and just kick back, but he said he couldn't, that he had important meetings.''

"You can understand that. He couldn't very well cancel them at the last minute without a more valid excuse. What you should get him to do is take a vacation. You two need to get away together.''

Sharon heard her out stoically. "Rachel phoned at three to say Trevor wouldn't be home for dinner. At four I got a call from the head of the accounting department. She asked if I knew where to reach Trevor. He hadn't been in the office today and they needed some important papers. She said she wouldn't have bothered me, but his secretary left early.''

After a stunned moment of silence, Kate tried to be reassuring. "That doesn't mean she went to meet Trevor.''

"Grow up, Kate. I have,'' Sharon said bleakly. "My marriage is finished.''

"You have to give him a chance to explain first!''

"I couldn't bear to look at him, knowing he's been lying to me all this time.''

"None of this adds up. Every marriage has problems, but I can't believe Trevor wouldn't try to work them out.''

"He doesn't love me anymore.'' Sharon buried her face in her hands and started to sob.

Kate patted her back, murmuring comforting words while she tried to figure out the true story. Trevor's behavior was at odds with everything she knew about him. Either he was a consummate actor, or there was another explanation.

When her sobs quieted Sharon said, "Can I stay here with you tonight? I can't go back to that house.''

"Of course you can stay," Kate assured her. "Why don't you take a nice relaxing bubble bath and get into bed. I'll give you a nightie."

"I don't want to put you out. I can sleep on the couch."

"You need a good night's rest," Kate told her. "I've slept on the couch lots of times when I've fallen asleep watching television."

After overriding Sharon's protests, Kate turned on the water in the tub. While the bubbles were foaming she laid out her best chiffon nightgown.

As Sharon started into the bathroom Kate said, "Will you be all right if I leave you alone for a short time? I was supposed to meet some friends."

"I'm sorry to have disrupted your life," Sharon said penitently. "Go ahead and keep your date. I'll be okay now."

"I'll be back soon." Kate left hurriedly, before Sharon asked questions about where she was going.

Kate was relieved to see lights in the Hamiltons' house. She hadn't relished waiting in the car for Trevor to return, although she'd been prepared to do just that.

He answered the doorbell immediately, looking worried. When he saw her, his dawning relief died. "Oh, hi, Kate. I thought you were Sharon. She isn't home and I'm getting concerned. It isn't like her to go out without even leaving a note telling me where she'd be."

"Sharon is at my house," Kate said quietly.

"What's she doing there?" He stared at her with a puzzled frown.

"May I come in? I want to talk to you."

His face paled. "Has something happened to Sharon?"

"Not the way you mean. She's left you, Trevor."

"*What*?" After a shocked moment he said, "Come inside."

Leading her into the living room he slumped into a chair, looking defeated. "I was a little on edge last night, but I can't believe Sharon would overreact like this."

"That isn't why she left you. Sharon thinks you're having an affair with your secretary. Are you, Trevor?" Kate asked bluntly.

"No!" His answer was explosive. "I've never been unfaithful to my wife."

"Then you have some tall explaining to do. Sharon knows you didn't go to work today, after you told her you had important meetings. She also found out that Rachel left early. To meet you?"

"Yes, but..." He put his head in his hands, groaning. "God, what a mess."

"Have you been seeing Rachel all those nights you were supposed to be working?"

"Some of them," he admitted.

"And you expect Sharon to believe you weren't fooling around? *I* don't believe that, and I defended you."

"I've been acting like a real jerk, but it isn't as bad as it sounds." He sighed. "It all started when I went to work for the Carriage House. I had serious doubts, but Sharon and Garrett were very persuasive, and I didn't want to live on Sharon's money." He gestured around the opulent room. "My salary at the agency couldn't cover all this."

"Garrett must really have wanted you. He wouldn't have kept you a week if you didn't pull your weight."

"I did a good job, but I hated it." Trevor got up to pace the room, hands thrust in his pockets. "Do you know what it's like to hate going to work every day? I missed the creativity of the advertising business, the brainstorming sessions, the excitement when we were pitching a new client. Sharon never realized what my work meant to me.''

''So in retaliation you got your excitement from Rachel.''

''I got understanding,'' he corrected her sternly. ''Our relationship developed gradually. When you spend long hours with a person, you get to be friends. I took her to dinner a couple of times after we'd worked late. We talked about movies and politics, places we've been, anything but Carriage House business. She could sense that I was unhappy there. Which is more than my wife did.''

''That's not fair. Sharon knew something was wrong, but you never told her what it was.''

''She would have talked me out of it,'' he answered wearily. ''According to Sharon, our life was perfect.''

''So you told Rachel your troubles instead, and she was sympathetic. Clever girl. Just how comforting was she?''

For the first time he looked uncomfortable. ''I never slept with her.''

Kate got the picture. Rachel was willing, probably eager, but Trevor didn't really want to have an affair. He was unhappy and frustrated, though, so he'd drifted into a reasonably chaste relationship with Rachel because she was the only one he could talk to.

''Everything seemed to come to a head yesterday at the party,'' he continued. ''I was thirty-five years old, a kind of milestone. I looked around at all my possessions and I felt trapped. I was doomed to spend the rest of my life doing something I hated.''

''Did you think you could keep on lying to Sharon forever?''

"I don't know what I thought. I only knew I couldn't go to work today. I drove halfway to San Francisco and back without finding any answer. At three o'clock I phoned Rachel and told her to tell Sharon I wouldn't be home for dinner."

"And Rachel suggested she meet you somewhere," Kate remarked cynically.

"Yes," he answered in a low voice. "We walked in Roxbury Park, and I took her to dinner. I swear to you that's all that happened."

"I believe you. Now all you have to do is convince Sharon. If you want to, that is. Maybe you'd be better off splitting up if your goals are so different."

"I couldn't bear to lose her. This has taught me a frightening lesson. I'll change completely if she'll take me back. I won't ever think about the ad business again. I'll be everything she wants me to be."

"You love her that much?"

"She's my whole world," he answered simply.

Kate had a lump in her throat. "Tell her that. And tell her everything else you've told me. I think you're due for a happy surprise."

"What if she refuses to see me?" he asked hesitantly.

Kate took her house key from her purse and handed it to him. "Let yourself in with this. I'll be home in about an hour."

After Trevor left she used the phone to call Garrett. When she told him the story he was completely dumbfounded.

"Why didn't he ever tell me how he felt?" he exclaimed.

"You and Sharon are pretty formidable," Kate replied ruefully.

"You knew about this, didn't you?" he demanded.

"No, but I had a hunch."

"Is Trevor there now? I want to talk to him."

"I sent him over to my house to straighten things out with Sharon. I hope she understands that she was partly responsible."

"I have a share in the guilt. I pressured him to take the job, too."

"Trevor says he's going to forget about his former career, but I wonder if he won't always have regrets," Kate said slowly.

"Don't worry. If he doesn't have sense enough to quit, I'll fire him," Garrett declared.

"That has to be his decision and Sharon's, but I do think he should start his own ad agency."

"What a terrific idea! Did you tell him that?"

"I mentioned it once. Right now he's only interested in patching things up with Sharon. I'll give them an hour alone together before I go home."

"Why don't you come over here for an hour, and then I'll go back with you?"

"No way." Kate laughed. "Time has a way of getting away from us. I'll meet you on neutral ground."

After lingering in a coffee shop, Kate and Garrett drove back to her apartment. They looked at each other apprehensively as she rang the bell.

"I hope Sharon is being sensible," Kate murmured.

"I do, too, but this thing really shook her up," Garrett said.

Their concern vanished when Trevor opened the door. All the lines were gone from his face and his taut body was relaxed. Sharon was sitting on the couch wearing Kate's nightgown and a negligee. She was a different woman from the distracted one who had arrived earlier.

"Did you two talk things out?" Kate asked.

"Trevor told me everything and we forgave each other," Sharon said softly. "I'll never try to run his life again."

He gazed adoringly at her pink cheeks and bright eyes. "I'm not expecting miracles," he teased.

"You'll see." She turned to her brother. "Trevor is quitting his job, Garrett."

"I know. Kate told me the whole story."

"Don't try to talk him out of it," Sharon said before he could continue. "I'm behind Trevor one hundred percent on this."

"You probably think I'm crazy," Trevor said defensively. "I'll only earn a fraction of what I was making at the Carriage House."

"I doubt that seriously," Garrett answered. "Ad agencies are very profitable. I expect yours to be a big success, especially when it gets around that you have the Carriage House for a client."

"You'd take a chance on me?" Trevor asked with dawning excitement.

"When it comes to business, I only gamble on sure things," Garrett said with a smile.

"This calls for a celebration," Sharon declared. "Do you have any champagne, Kate?"

"I'm afraid not. Will cooking sherry do?" she asked.

"It will taste like champagne," Sharon answered, gazing at her husband with stars in her eyes.

The atmosphere was very festive as they sat around discussing plans for Trevor's new venture. Kate couldn't have been happier for them, but as the hour grew later she had trouble suppressing a yawn.

Sharon finally noticed her struggles. "It's time we got out of here and let Kate get some sleep. I'll get dressed."

Trevor's eyes held a gleam of anticipation as they swept over his wife's enticingly clad body. "Maybe Kate could just lend you a coat," he said casually.

Sharon started to object until their eyes met. "That *would* save time," she murmured.

"I'm sure Kate appreciates your concern for her." Garrett laughed. "Take the day off tomorrow, Trevor."

"I'll be in, but it might not be before noon." Trevor grinned.

Garrett prepared to leave soon after his sister and brother-in-law had gone. "I'd like to stay, but you do look tired, honey," he told Kate.

"It's been a full day," she admitted.

"The best Monday I've ever spent." He took her in his arms and kissed her tenderly, then with increasing warmth. Finally he dragged his mouth away unwillingly. "I'd better go or I'll be here all night."

"We do have to work tomorrow," she answered with equal reluctance.

"Unfortunately. Try to get home early tomorrow night, angel."

She looked at him blankly, forgetting her date with Ian for the moment. After her memory was jogged, incredulity followed. "You want me to keep my date?"

"It's up to you. Not if you're too tired."

Anger swept through her. What did it take to convince Garrett that he was all she would ever want? If last night and today hadn't done it, nothing would.

"I'm sure by tomorrow night I'll be ready and eager," she replied coolly.

"Good night, Kate," he said quietly after kissing her cheek.

Kate didn't want to go out with Ian or anyone else that Tuesday night. She was tired and cross, but she made a determined effort to be pleasant. After all, it wasn't Ian's fault.

He was so delighted to be with her that she began to have a good time in spite of her initial dark mood. They went to a reception at an art gallery, and then on to a party given by friends of his. The guests were amusing, and she and Ian laughed a lot.

When they pulled up in front of her house he didn't get out immediately. Turning toward her, he said, "I had a really great time tonight, but that's no surprise. I always do when I'm with you. I hope you feel the same about me."

"I do, Ian," she answered.

He laughed slightly. "I always imagined when a woman said that to me she'd be wearing a white veil and carrying orange blossoms."

"And then you'd wake up in a cold sweat," she teased.

"Do I give that impression?"

She tried to prevent him from becoming serious. "No one would blame you. You were born to make a lot of women happy."

"I'm very fond of you, Kate." His voice was soft.

"That's sweet," she answered vaguely.

"You're more than just a fun date to me. You know that, don't you?" He leaned forward and kissed her.

Kate left a pang of guilt. She was fond of Ian, too, but that was as far as it went. If he was really falling in love with her, she had to put a stop to it. He was too nice a person to take advantage of while Garrett made up his mind—one way or the other.

"You're a really fine person," she began hesitantly.

"I don't like the sound of that." He gave her a crooked smile. "It's usually followed by a but."

"Any woman would be proud to have you interested in her."

"But not you?"

"I'm not in love with you," she said helplessly. "I wish I were."

"Is there someone else?"

"Yes," she answered honestly.

"He's a lucky guy. Are you going to marry him?"

"I don't know," she replied in a low voice.

"Then you can't be all that sure it's love. Why don't I hang around till you decide?"

She couldn't tell him it was Garrett who wasn't sure. "You deserve better," she said unhappily.

"They don't come any better than you." His voice was husky.

Before she could answer he got out of the car and came around to the passenger side. As they walked toward her apartment house, Ian put his arm around Kate's shoulders and hugged her close.

"I don't intend to let you go without a struggle. Is there any chance I could buy this guy off?" he joked.

"I doubt it." She smiled. "He's already overstocked with worldly goods."

"Well if the worst happens, maybe you can adopt me. Don't laugh, it's not such a bad deal. You wouldn't have to teach me table manners, and my college education is already paid for."

When they reached her door, Ian's levity vanished. He took her in his arms and kissed her with unmistakable desire. Kate submitted, but she couldn't return his ardor.

After a few moments he released her. "Well, at least you didn't push me away," he said wryly. "I'll call you tomorrow, honey."

* * *

Garrett hadn't made any attempt to conceal his presence near Kate's house. Although his car was parked a few doors away, it was noteworthy enough to draw attention. The fact that neither Kate nor Ian had noticed him deepened the scowl that had formed when he witnessed the kiss between them.

After Ian had driven away, Garrett got out, slamming the door hard enough to be heard a block away. He strode furiously into the apartment building and leaned on Kate's doorbell.

She had just taken off her dress when the insistent ringing sounded. Pulling on a robe, she ran to the front door and opened it.

"What's wrong, Ian? Did you—" She stopped abruptly on seeing Garrett. "What are you doing here at this hour?"

"It *is* rather late. You must have had a good time tonight," he remarked with controlled fury.

"As a matter of fact, I did," she replied coolly.

"So I noticed! But isn't making out in a car rather juvenile? Or is that one of those high-school practices you always wanted to try?"

"*You* were the one who told me to find out what I missed," she flared. "I was only following instructions."

Garrett towered over her. "What else did you do with Ian?"

"None of your business! You had no right to spy on me."

"I was in plain sight if you'd cared to look. You and your boyfriend were too wrapped up in each other to notice."

"We had no reason to suspect we were under surveillance," she said indignantly.

"Would you still have let him kiss you and put his hands all over you?"

"Oh, for heaven's sake, Garrett," she said disgustedly. "You're making a federal case out of nothing."

"I suppose you'll deny that you let him kiss you again when he took you inside?"

"Why should I deny it?"

"Did you kiss him like you kiss me?" His body was as rigid as a steel rod.

"What do you want from me, Garrett?" she asked slowly, her anger fading. "Or don't you know yourself?"

He reached out and drew her into a smothering embrace. "All I know is, I can't stand to see you with another man. When Ian kissed you, I wanted to pull him out of the car and beat him to a pulp."

"It wasn't a very passionate kiss," Kate panted, struggling to breathe.

"I don't want any man to touch you but me. Marry me, Kate, before I make a complete fool of myself."

Her first reaction was overwhelming joy. Then caution set in. "Are you *sure*, Garrett? Jealousy isn't a very sound basis for marriage."

"I can give you a couple of hundred more reasons, starting with the fact that I can't live without you."

She looked at him searchingly. "If you hadn't seen Ian kiss me, would you still have proposed?"

He smiled tenderly. "Why do you think I was waiting for you to come home? Just the thought of you with another man drove me so crazy I knew I couldn't be unselfish anymore."

"Oh, Garrett, I'm so glad you stopped being virtuous!"

He swung her into his arms, chuckling deeply. "Is that your definition of my behavior?"

Kate put her arms around his neck as he carried her into the bedroom. "If it hadn't been for those little lapses, I would have given up hope of ever trapping you," she said mischievously.

He set her gently on the bed and stared down at her, his face sobering. "I hope it's not the other way around."

She untied his tie and began unbuttoning his shirt. "Do you think you'll be sure of me by our fiftieth anniversary? Or will you suspect me of having a secret yen for some cute doctor in the geriatric ward?"

Garrett's face relaxed as he parted her robe. "The guy will be lucky if I let him examine you. You'll still have a body that will make men lose control." He nuzzled aside her bra and curled his tongue around her rosy nipple.

They undressed each other slowly, pausing for deep kisses and arousing caresses. When they were completely nude Garrett took her in his arms, fitting their bodies together.

"My better half," he murmured. "I need you to make me whole."

"We need each other, darling."

They merged joyfully, achieving total completion. Shared pleasure vibrated through their joined bodies, fusing them into one entity that soared to the stars and back. The experience was so moving that they clung tightly to each other afterward, unwilling to break the bond.

Much later, Garrett said drowsily, "What are you thinking about?"

"How nice it is to have you here like this," she answered contentedly. "Are you going to stay all night?"

"You better believe it." He wrapped his legs more closely around hers. "And every night from now on."

She smiled in the darkness. "You're moving in? I don't know if I have enough closet space."

"I meant we're going to be together every night. Let's get married tomorrow."

Kate laughed. "For a man who couldn't make up his mind, you're certainly in a hurry all of a sudden."

"I don't want to take a chance on anything happening to stop us."

"Nothing will ever come between us." She stroked his cheek lovingly.

After they kissed tenderly and murmured promises to each other, Garrett returned to the subject of their wedding. "Let's set a date, angel, so we can begin to make plans. I'll have to arrange for someone to take over while we're on our honeymoon."

She sighed happily. "That sounds so definite."

"It won't be, if you don't pick a date."

"Well, let's see. The foundation will be making a decision on my grant this month. I have to be here for that."

"And I have some important cases coming before the grand jury in a couple of weeks," Garrett said thoughtfully.

"How about the fifteenth of next month. I'll be free by then. How about you?"

"I think I can fit you into my schedule," he teased.

"Give it your best shot because *I'm* getting married on the fifteenth. If you're not available I'll just have to make do with a handy substitute."

"Don't even think about it, unless you want a seriously damaged bridegroom."

"We'll have to do something about that violent streak of yours," she joked. "Where shall we go on our honeymoon?"

His hand moved sensuously over her body. "Do we have to discuss it now?" he murmured.

She turned to face him, her eyes luminous in the darkness. "Not if you can think of something better to do."

Sharon was overjoyed when they told her the news. She insisted on giving them an engagement party.

"You just got through having that big birthday party for Trevor," Kate protested. They were having lunch at the club while the men were at a baseball game.

"So what?" Sharon brushed Kate's objection aside. "This is a red-letter occasion. Garrett is finally getting married—and to someone I approve of." She laughed. "That in itself calls for a celebration."

"True," Kate agreed impishly. "You could have been stuck with Lorna."

"Garrett would never be that brain-dead. Lorna's going to explode when she hears the news. I suppose I'll have to invite her to the party."

"Why? Garrett has gone with other women. Are you going to invite all of them?"

"Lorna's case is a little different. Our families see each other and we have a lot of the same friends. It would be sort of a slap in the face to exclude her. It's your party, though. If you're uncomfortable about having her there, I won't invite her."

"No, go ahead. I understand. But I'm beginning to wish I'd taken Garrett up on it when he wanted to get married immediately," Kate said slowly.

"Premarital jitters?" Sharon joked.

"Just jitters." Kate's expression was sober. "I have an uneasy feeling that everything is too perfect to last. I'm afraid something is bound to happen to spoil it."

"Everybody feels that way when they've found the man of their dreams," Sharon said softly.

"At least you don't have anything to worry about anymore. Everything's coming up roses. Trevor has a new business, and you'll have an exciting career."

"Eventually." Sharon's face was dreamy. "I intend to get my degree, but I won't be going to work immediately. Trevor and I are going to have a baby."

"Fantastic!" Kate exclaimed. "I've always wanted to be an aunt."

"So have I. How about returning the favor?"

"Do you mind if I wait till I'm married?" Kate grinned. "I'm the old-fashioned type."

In spite of Kate's fears, nothing happened to mar the happiness she and Garrett shared. Her grant seemed assured, and Garrett had been approached to run for public office. In addition to their busy schedules they had to make plans for the wedding, but that was pure pleasure. After the big event they would have two glorious weeks in Tahiti for a honeymoon.

Kate was in a perpetual glow that was especially pronounced the night of the engagement party. She looked ravishing in a new rose-colored satin dress with a deep décolleté neckline. The long earrings that dangled almost to her shoulders matched the sparkle in her hazel eyes.

"You look sensational," Garrett said when he came to pick her up that night. "Do we really have to go to the party? I could have a much better time here with you."

She evaded his reaching arms and picked up her evening purse. "These are your friends," she pointed out.

"Let's stay home and make love. We can always make new friends."

Kate laughed. "I wouldn't mind discarding a couple of your old ones."

Sharon had outdone herself. Red and white roses filled the house with fragrance and color, a sumptuous buffet was laid out in the dining room, and a four-piece orchestra played in the large den where a portable dance floor had been laid down.

"No balloons and confetti?" Garrett joked, glancing around the elegant rooms.

"It isn't New Year's Eve," Sharon chided.

He put his arm around Kate and gazed deeply into her eyes. "It's every holiday rolled into one for us."

They were too engrossed in each other to notice Lorna watching them from the hall. Naked anger ravaged her face in the unguarded moment.

"You win some, you lose some." Foster had sauntered over to her.

"This is just a temporary setback." Her eyes never wavered from Garrett and Kate. "Their marriage will never last."

"There comes a time when you have to be realistic. I've known Garrett for a lot of years, and I've never seen him this sappy over a woman."

"Garrett was crazy about *me* until she came along," Lorna answered shrilly. "God knows what perverted acts she performed to get him away from me."

"I'll bet *you'd* like to know," Foster said mockingly.

"You're disgusting," she snapped.

"We're two of a kind, kid. Both of us would empty out our bag of dirty tricks to get what we want. The difference is, I know when the odds are stacked against me."

"We'll see," she muttered, stalking away.

As the guests of honor, Kate and Garrett didn't get to spend much time together. They circulated in different directions, accepting congratulations as they tried to have at least a few words with every guest.

Lorna bided her time, waiting until she could get Garrett alone. His smile became fixed as she approached and put her hand on his arm.

"I suppose congratulations are in order, but I always hoped I'd be the one receiving them," she said wistfully.

"You will be," he answered kindly.

"Only if I'm willing to settle for second-best."

"Be honest, Lorna. You weren't in love with me."

"How can you say that?" She gave him a wounded look.

"Because it's true. We were compatible and I fit your requirements, but the spark wasn't there for either of us."

"You're wrong! It will always be there for me." Her voice rose.

Garrett was aware of the covert glances being cast their way. "This discussion is pointless," he said with distaste.

"I'm sorry if the truth makes you uncomfortable," she replied bitterly.

"Did you come here for a confrontation?" he demanded.

After a look at his set face, Lorna changed tactics. "I would never do anything to make you unhappy. If I can't have your love, I hope we can at least remain friends."

His stony expression relaxed. "I'd like that. Our friendship goes back a long way."

"Oh, Garrett, I think I'm going to cry." She fluttered her lashes rapidly.

"Not here, you're not," he muttered. Putting an arm around her shoulders he hustled her out of the crowded room.

Kate was standing in the dining room with a group of people when she saw Garrett lead Lorna into a room across the hall. She continued to smile, even after he closed the door.

Any number of reasons could explain their actions, Kate told herself. Lorna wanted to make a phone call and Garrett was showing her where the telephone was. Lorna had a headache and he was getting her an aspirin. The possibilities were infinite.

As soon as Garrett closed the door, Lorna's incipient tears vanished. "Thanks for getting me out of there. I wouldn't want to make a fool of myself in front of all our friends."

"Are you all right now?" he asked.

"As right as I'll ever be, I suppose."

"Stay here if you like. I have to get back to the party," he said evenly.

"Wait, Garrett! She clutched at his sleeve. "I have something to say to you."

He tried with only partial success to control his impatience. "There isn't any more to say."

"Yes, there is. I know you think you're in love with Kate, but—"

"I *am* in love with her!"

"For now. But marriage isn't all moonlight and roses. She's an outsider. She won't fit into your life-style."

"I've witnessed bad taste before, but nothing like this," he said coldly.

"You're too blind to see it now, but it could happen," Lorna insisted. "I just wanted to tell you I'll be waiting."

"You're really sick!" he exclaimed, staring at her in disbelief.

"Just remember. I'll be waiting," she repeated, throwing her arms around his neck.

Kate's eyes kept returning to the door across the hall. When it remained closed she stopped making excuses. Who was she kidding? Lorna and Garrett weren't discussing the size of the national debt in there.

Making a polite excuse to the people she was with, Kate marched across the hall with smoldering eyes. She opened the door to find Garrett and Lorna in each other's arms.

They drew apart and Garrett stared at her speechlessly. Lorna, however, looked pleased with herself.

"I do hope you're not going to make a scene," she drawled.

"Of course not," Kate answered. "Why should I?"

Lorna was disconcerted by her calm. "I thought you might be upset to find Garrett kissing me so passionately."

Ignoring the strangled sound he made, Kate laughed merrily. "Is that what you call a passionate kiss? My goodness, I do feel sorry for you. Your relationship must have been awfully tepid." She held out her hand to Garrett. "Come on, darling. People are asking for you."

Lorna's face was a study in rage and frustration as Garrett followed Kate silently.

When he was alone with her in the hall he said, "You have to let me explain. What you saw in there wasn't what it looked like."

"Nothing could have been clearer," she answered.

"I don't know how to say this without sounding like a cad, but Lorna was the instigator. I was trying to get away from her."

"I know that," Kate said calmly.

He looked at her in surprise. "You believe me?"

She smiled and put her arms around his neck. "You can't help it if you make women lust after you. I'd like to instigate something with you, myself."

"You're not angry?" he asked uncertainly.

"Not at you. But if that witch makes a pass at you one more time, I'm **goin**g to ground her with her own broomstick."

"I love you," Garrett said, tightening his arms around her and burying his face in her hair.

"I know," Kate replied smugly.

Chapter Eleven

Foster Gray dropped in unexpectedly at Garrett's office a few days after the party. Garrett was mildly surprised. Usually they met for lunch or at a gym for handball. He had no reason to suspect the visit was anything but social, however. They started out discussing the recent engagement party.

"You've really got the world by the tail, buddy boy," Foster commented. "A gorgeous girl, all the money in the world, even fame in the offing."

Garrett looked at him quizzically. "Fame?"

"Well, prominence anyway. You're still thinking of going into politics, aren't you?"

"It's been suggested," Garrett admitted. "That doesn't necessarily mean I could get elected."

Foster's mouth twisted sardonically. "Have you ever failed to get anything you wanted?"

"It wasn't handed to me," Garrett answered quietly.

"Not another lecture, please. I have a hangover."

Garrett gazed at him steadily. "Is this a social visit, or did you have a reason for coming?"

"I never could fool you," Foster said wryly.

"I suppose you want to borrow money again." Garrett sighed. "Aren't any of your various enterprises ever profitable?"

"The latest one was, but you might say I ran into restraint of trade."

"Spare me the details." Garrett took his checkbook out of the desk drawer. "How much?"

"Twenty-five thousand dollars."

Garrett looked up. "Maybe you'd better go into detail, after all."

"I need to hire a good lawyer."

"What for?"

"It's a bum rap, but you of all people know about the judicial system," Foster answered evasively. "The case will probably drag through the courts for months."

"Who is suing you, and why?"

"I'm not exactly being sued."

Garrett leaned back in his chair and folded his arms. "Suppose you tell me the whole story from the beginning."

"It's an out-and-out case of harassment. The police claim I'm operating a prostitution ring."

Garrett stared at him incredulously. "You were arrested?"

"Like a common thief! You'd think the vice squad would go after *real* criminals."

"Prostitution *is* a crime."

"Not like selling drugs or sticking up a liquor store. Besides, I'm innocent," Foster said hastily. "I run a legitimate escort service."

"Stuff it, Foster! We both know what services your 'escorts' perform."

"I'm not admitting anything, but what would be so wrong if they did? A bunch of lonely women get their kicks with a good-looking guy who isn't going to beat them up and rob them afterward. Isn't that better than having them cruise the bars and pick up weirdos?"

"My God, I never heard prostitution described as a social service!"

"Who the hell are you to judge?" Foster flared.

"Someone who knows the difference between right and wrong. There are acceptable ways to make money—and there are your ways."

"Don't hand me that moralistic garbage! Only a guy who cut his teeth on a solid-gold teething ring can afford your kind of scruples."

"I wasn't aware that scruples were the sole privilege of the rich," Garrett answered scathingly.

"You wouldn't be so holier-than-thou if you'd ever had to scrounge for money. Do you know what it's like to owe everybody from your tailor to the corner liquor store? I've had to sneak into my apartment so the manager couldn't see me and hit me up for the rent."

Garrett gazed at him impassively. "Cheer up. If you go to jail, your room and board will be free."

"That's not funny! I'm in a real jam."

"I'm glad you understand *that* much anyhow."

"Okay, so you think I'm irresponsible. But you'll help me out, won't you? Somebody recommended this hot-shot lawyer, but the shyster insists on his money up front."

"That was a wise move in your case."

"Come on, Garrett. Don't keep me twisting in the wind. I'm your old pal, remember?"

"I've pulled you out of a lot of scrapes in the name of friendship," Garrett said slowly. "I told myself you were just immature, that you'd settle down some day. I never realized what a warped sense of values you have."

"You want me to beg. Is that it?" Foster sneered.

"I want you to be a man instead of a juvenile delinquent," Garrett said sternly. "I can see now that I didn't do you a favor by bailing you out of your endless messes."

"You're turning me down?" Foster asked in disbelief. "You'd let me go to jail?"

"It might give you the jolt you need," Garrett said wearily.

"You're enjoying this." Foster leaped up and glared at Garrett across the desk. "You'd never miss the money, but you like seeing me squirm. Guys like you make me sick!"

"The feeling is entirely mutual. You'd better leave, Foster."

"I'm not slinking out of here with my tail between my legs."

"I'll be happy to assist you to the door."

"I wouldn't be in such a hurry if I were you. I can be a mean enemy."

"That wouldn't be much different from having you as a friend," Garrett answered contemptuously.

"Oh, yeah? How would you like everybody to know how you met your blushing bride-to-be?"

Garrett's face might have been carved out of stone. "None of this concerns Kate."

"What's the matter, Garrett? Are you ashamed to have people find out she came to me looking for a stud?" Foster taunted.

"That's a damn lie and you know it!"

"I wonder how many people would think so after hearing the story."

"I told you to leave Kate out of this." Garrett's voice was steely.

"Sure. I'm a reasonable man. It will only cost you twenty-five big ones."

"Do you honestly think I'd pay blackmail?"

"That's an ugly word. I prefer to think of it as payment to an advisor. I'm advising you that Kate isn't the only one who could get hurt. If this got around you could kiss off your chance for public office. Voters expect their elected officials to be squeaky-clean these days. The twenty-five grand will keep all of us out of the papers."

Garrett's expression was unreadable. "You had your game plan all figured out before you came here, didn't you?"

Foster shrugged. "You forced me to use it."

"It's never your fault, is it?"

"We're wasting time," Foster said impatiently. "Write the check and I'll get out of here."

"Sorry, *old chum*," Garrett stressed the words sarcastically. "You ran your bluff on the wrong man."

"I'm not bluffing," Foster warned.

"You'd better be, because I'll tell you what would happen. If you ever mention Kate's name, I'll tell the vice-squad boys to see what else they can dig up on you. I seem to remember a shipment of expensive watches you received right about the time the market was flooded with counterfeits."

"I was only a partner in that deal, just an investor actually. As far as I knew, those watches were genuine."

"Your partner might tell a different story if the police start questioning him. That's not really vice-squad business, but they like to make brownie points with the grand jury. They'll be all over you like fleas on a tall dog."

Foster licked his lips nervously. "You wouldn't really put them on my case."

"Damn straight I would," Garrett assured him. "Get out of my office and stay out of my life, Foster."

Garrett didn't tell Kate about Foster's visit. He seemed a little preoccupied when he phoned her that evening, but she attributed it to all the things he had on his mind. They were both working at top speed so they could take time off for a honeymoon. Although they spoke on the phone every evening, often they didn't see each other for several days at a time.

One night Kate's doorbell rang soon after she'd gotten home. Thinking Garrett had managed to finish up early for once, she opened the door eagerly. Her smile faded when she saw Foster.

He looked back at her warily. "May I come in?"

"I suppose so." When he followed her into the living room she tried to make up for her ungraciousness. "What brings you here? Were you looking for Garrett?"

He seemed more relaxed suddenly. "No, I came to see you."

Concealing her surprise she said, "I'm sorry I can only offer you coffee to drink."

"I don't care for anything, thanks."

"Would you like to sit down?" she asked tentatively.

"You're probably wondering why I'm here," he said, guessing correctly.

"Well, yes," she admitted.

"I could waste a lot of time in small talk, but there is no easy way to lead up to this. I need twenty-five thousand dollars, Kate."

She stared at him as though he had sprouted another head. "Why come to me?"

"Because if I don't get it, I'll be forced to tell the police you were one of my clients."

"The police!" she gasped. "What do they have to do with it?"

Foster smiled sardonically. "They claim the men working for me provided more than escort services."

"Garrett suspected as much!" Kate exclaimed. "That's why he volunteered to take me to the reunion. He realized I wasn't looking for anything like that."

"The fact remains that you used a dating bureau that's under investigation. I imagine your prestigious institute would take a dim view of one of their scientists being mixed up in a scandal."

"You'd try to drag me down with you?" How could anyone sink that low? "Suppose I deny the whole thing? It would be your word against mine—and I'm a lot more credible."

"But I have proof," he answered. "I made a photostat of your check before I cashed it. That's a common practice of mine. You never know what's going to come in handy."

"You're really despicable." She stared at him with loathing.

"Name-calling won't get us anywhere, so let's get down to business. Either you give me the money or risk losing your job."

That was a distinct possibility, but even if she managed to salvage her position, she'd surely lose the grant she'd worked so hard for. Something like this would tip the balance in favor of the other candidate.

"Even if I were willing to pay you off, I don't have that kind of money," she said hopelessly.

"You could get it from Garrett."

She looked at him with sudden speculation. "Why didn't you go to him yourself? He's your friend. I'm not."

"I did ask Garrett, but he said he couldn't give it to me because of being head of the grand jury. It might be considered a conflict of interest. You'd better not tell him I came to you," Foster warned. "If he doesn't know what the money is for, he's in the clear."

Kate was too distracted to question his feeble reasoning. "I couldn't ask Garrett for that much money without telling him what it was for."

"Call it a wedding present. Or say your mother needs an operation. You're a smart girl. You'll think of something."

"I won't lie to Garrett," she said adamantly. "If you're determined to try to wreck my reputation, I'll just have to take my chances on having people believe me instead of you."

"I hoped I wouldn't have to do this, but you're forcing me to fight dirty."

"What do you call what you've been doing?" she asked scornfully.

"Merely a warm-up. If you don't get me the money I'll say Garrett was one of my stable of studs. That he did it for kicks, because it was kinky."

"Even *you* can't be crazy enough to think anyone would believe that."

"You'd be surprised. A lot of people are always ready to believe the worst. They'd sure as hell wonder what he gave you for your money."

"You wouldn't do that to your best friend," she whispered in horror.

"Not unless I have to. We're talking survival here. You think *your* reputation would suffer? His would be in shreds. What do you suppose this would do to business at the Carriage House?''

Kate's whole world was crashing down around her. Foster's threats were monstrous, but she knew he would carry them out. He was like a cornered rat, vicious and dangerous. Her own situation wasn't enviable, but Garrett would be destroyed. How could she save him? The answer caused her heart to twist cruelly.

"None of this has to happen if you get me the money," Foster coaxed. "You can see I hold all the cards."

"Not quite. Your advantage disappears if I call off the wedding. Sure, you can go ahead with your lies, but what will it get you? You still won't have the money and you'll have made a powerful enemy. Garrett will find some way to make you pay."

His confidence vanished as he looked at her white face. "You wouldn't call it off. Garrett is worth millions."

Her smile held no mirth. "How typical of you to put a price tag on sacrifice. I'm giving Garrett up because I love him."

"He won't let you do it," Foster said uneasily.

"I have no intention of telling him the real reason."

"You're just going to say, Sorry, I changed my mind? Give me a break!"

"Let me worry about how to do it. I'm a smart girl," she repeated his earlier words mockingly.

He stared at her, searching for signs of weakness without finding any. "I believe you're serious."

"That's the first glimmer of intelligence you've shown."

"Be reasonable, Kate. It's only money. Garrett is loaded, and you admit you love him."

"Do you think I don't know this would only be the beginning? You'd blackmail me forever."

"No! I'll give you back your check."

"After making another copy. My marriage would be doomed from the start. You'd bleed me dry, and Garrett would never trust me again if he found out I lied to him."

"He won't," Foster insisted. "This will be the end of it."

"You've seen to that," Kate answered bitterly. "Get out of my sight, Foster. You're polluting the air."

After he'd gone, Kate tried to find another solution, but she knew there wasn't any. It was clear now that Foster had tried to get the money from Garrett and been turned down. But not for the reason he'd given. She could never get the money from Garrett herself without an explanation. And if she proposed calling off the wedding, even temporarily, he'd flatly refuse. She would have to deceive him after all.

The decision was painful, and carrying it out was even harder. Kate began by finding reasons for not seeing Garrett that week. He wasn't happy about it, yet he accepted her excuses. The weekend was what gave her a problem. They always spent Saturday and Sunday together.

When she made up a story about having to fly to San Francisco to see a relative she invented, Garrett lost patience. "For the whole weekend? I haven't seen you in days."

"I'm sorry, darling, but I haven't seen my cousin in years. She came out from the east for a wedding. If I don't fly up there, who knows when we'll have another chance to get together?"

"I thought Aunt Jen was your only relative."

"On my father's side. Marsha is my mother's sister's daughter." That didn't ring true even to Kate's ears, but Garrett was too disappointed to pursue the subject.

"Okay," he sighed. "I'll go with you."

"No, you can't do that! Uh, Aunt Jen is going with me. We'll be sharing a hotel room. Besides, it wouldn't be any fun for you."

"Is that what you think?" His voice deepened. "I miss you, funny face."

Kate's heart plunged. How could she live without Garrett? "I'll call you when I get back," she said brightly.

"What time does your plane get in? I'll pick you up Sunday night. At least we can salvage a few hours out of the weekend," he murmured.

"I . . . we . . . we're not coming back until Monday morning. I'll take a cab right to work."

"How much time do you need with your cousin?" he demanded. "I'm beginning to think you don't want to be with me."

"Please don't be difficult, Garrett." She was close to tears.

He could hear the tension in her voice. "I'm sorry, honey. I'm being selfish. In just a few weeks I'll have you all to myself."

Kate couldn't trust herself to continue the conversation. "Goodbye, my love," she whispered brokenly.

Kate realized a showdown was inevitable. She couldn't hold Garrett off forever. Matters came to a head when she was most vulnerable after a grueling day at work. Garrett arrived at her apartment without warning.

The blessed sight of him was almost her undoing. He looked so handsome and vital. She longed to throw herself in his arms and feel every taut muscle in his splendid body.

Biting her lip, she turned away. "I wasn't expecting you. Why didn't you phone?"

"What kind of a greeting is that?" He pulled her into his arms, fulfilling her wish. "I didn't call because you always give me some reason why we can't get together. Not tonight, though. We're going to forget about work and everything else while I make mad, passionate love to you."

Kate knew the moment of truth had arrived. She forced herself to draw away. "We have to talk, Garrett."

"Later," he said, reaching for her again.

"No, now." She turned her back, unable to watch his face. "I can't marry you."

"Is this some kind of joke?"

"I'm really sorry," she whispered.

He seized her arm and whirled her around. "What's happened, Kate?"

She bowed her head. "I don't love you."

He jerked her chin up and stared at her tortured face. "You don't mean that."

"You were right all along, Garrett. I didn't have enough experience to distinguish love from passion."

He drew in his breath sharply. "You're just having an attack of nerves, angel. All brides get cold feet at the last minute. A lot of grooms, too." His laughter had a forced sound.

"It's more than that. There's someone else."

Garrett's fingers bit into her shoulders. "Is that why you've been so elusive lately? You've been seeing another man?"

"Yes." Her voice was almost inaudible.

"Who is it?"

"Palmer Wesley." As Garrett made an incredulous sound she said, "He called and apologized for his behavior that night. He said he'd been thinking about me all this time."

"And you believed him?"

"I guess I wanted to. He asked me to have lunch with him, and I didn't see anything wrong with that."

"In spite of the fact that you were engaged to me?"

"It wasn't like a date. If I hadn't gone, he would have thought I rejected his apology."

"It wouldn't do to hurt his delicate feelings," Garrett said sarcastically. "Palmer is so sensitive."

"You've always misjudged him."

"No, *you* have! If you're having second thoughts about marrying me, I'll have to accept the fact. But I'm damned if I'll let that slime bucket take advantage of you again."

"You can't stop me from seeing him."

"When are you going to grow up, Kate?" he asked roughly. "The guy wants only one thing from you, and after he gets it he'll discard you like a wad of used bubble gum."

"You're wrong. Palmer loves me. I can tell."

A nerve throbbed at Garrett's temple. "Has he already gotten what he wants?"

This was worse than anything she'd feared. Why didn't Garrett just storm out and stop tormenting her? The touch of his hands was destroying her willpower. In another minute she'd break down and beg him to make love to her.

Taking a deep breath, she forced herself to say the one thing that would drive him away. "Palmer and I are going away for the weekend."

After a moment of pulsing silence Garrett said flatly, "I don't believe it."

"I didn't want to tell you, but you forced me to. Does that convince you that we're in love?"

His mouth curled sardonically. "You think all the men who take women to motels are in love with them?"

"It isn't like that with us! We aren't going to a motel."
She couldn't bear to have Garrett think she was indulging
in a cheap affair.

"Oh, really? Where are you going?"

"Well, we . . . it's none of your business," she flared.

"You don't honestly intend to do this. It's not like you,
Kate," he said more gently. "Why do you want me to
believe you've changed so radically?"

Garrett mustn't start to wonder! "If you must know,
we're going to the Sea View Inn."

It was a small hotel in Malibu on the way to Garrett's
beach house, the first place that came to mind.

His jaw clenched, but he answered almost lightly,
"That's my neighborhood. Maybe you could drop in for
a drink."

"Please, Garrett, don't make it any worse," she said
wretchedly.

"I thought I was taking the news rather well. No tears,
very few jeers."

"You'd better leave."

"I suppose you're right. What more is there to say?"
He paused with his hand on the doorknob. "Are you sure
you've given this enough thought, Kate?"

"You'll never know how much." She sighed.

All the joy went out of Kate's life when she sent Garrett away. Even the work she loved failed to blunt the
pain. The lab was simply a place to go when she got up
in the morning. Saturday and Sunday would be almost
unbearable. The weekend Garrett thought she was
spending with Palmer.

A touch of uneasiness penetrated her misery. Garrett
knew where she was supposed to be going. Was it con-
ceivable that he'd phone to see if they were registered? If
he found out she'd lied to him they'd have another con-

frontation, and Kate knew she couldn't go through that again.

The safest solution would be to take a room at the inn for the weekend. That would satisfy Garrett if he decided to check up on her. The only drawback was that she'd have to make the reservation in the name of Mr. and Mrs. Palmer Wesley. Just the thought of it made her ill, but it couldn't be helped. What difference did it make really, in light of all the other things that had happened to her?

On Friday night after work, Kate went home and packed a bag with jeans and sweaters and several books. Her spirits lifted slightly at the prospect of a change of scenery. Everything in the apartment reminded her of Garrett. Maybe long walks along the beach would enable her to sleep without dreaming of him.

The Sea View Inn was comfortable, if not luxurious. Kate's oceanfront room had adequate reading lamps on both of the nightstands, and a bathroom with a shower over the tub.

The beach outside the window was too reminiscent of Garrett's house, so she drew the drapes and went to take a shower. Standing under the pelting water for long minutes helped to loosen her taut shoulder and neck muscles.

After putting on the flannel nightgown she'd brought because nights at the beach were chilly, Kate pulled her hair back with a ribbon and smoothed lotion on her face.

By the time she turned back the spread and got into bed, her tense body was more relaxed. Getting away had been a good idea. The only thing here to remind her of Garrett was the soothing sound of the surf. They'd spent many blissful nights lying in bed listening to it, twined in each other's arms. Kate quickly opened the book on her lap.

As she began to unwind, sheer exhaustion took over. The words on the page blurred and her eyelids drooped. She was dozing off when a loud banging at the door startled her awake. It sounded so urgent that she thought there must be some emergency. Jumping out of bed, she ran to the door in her bare feet.

Garrett pushed his way inside as soon as she turned the knob. His face was haggard. "I won't let you do it," he stated.

She simply stared at him. "What are you doing here?"

"I've come to take you home, whether you like it or not."

"I thought...I never dreamed you'd actually come here."

"I had to stop you from doing something you'd regret the rest of your life. In spite of what you believe, you're not thinking clearly."

As the shock wore off she pulled herself together. "You have no right to interfere. Please leave."

"You're coming with me if I have to carry you out," he answered grimly.

"You're ruining everything." She twisted her fingers together distractedly. "You have to get out of here."

"I doubt that your boyfriend is the physical type, but if he wants to take offense I'll be glad to thrash the matter out with him." Garrett glanced around the room for the first time. "Where is lover boy?"

Kate was tempted to say Palmer was in the bathroom, but no light shone under the door. "He, uh, he isn't here yet."

Garrett frowned. "You didn't come together?"

"No, Palmer had a meeting, a business meeting. He had to see an important client, so I came ahead in my own car."

"He's more interested in money than he is in you?" Garrett asked incredulously. "Doesn't that tell you what kind of man he is?"

"It was something that couldn't be helped. I understood that."

"Won't *anything* bring you to your senses?"

"He'll be here later," she insisted. "And I'd appreciate it if you aren't. Will you please go now?"

Garrett's eyes narrowed as he took a closer look at her. Then his gaze wandered to the stack of books on the bedside table.

"Let me get this straight," he said slowly. "You're expecting Palmer tonight? Not tomorrow morning?"

"I already told you he's coming soon."

"That's very strange."

"What is?" she asked warily.

"Usually when a woman goes away for the weekend with a man, she takes her sexiest nightgown—even if she doesn't expect to wear it very long."

Kate clutched the front of her high-necked flannel gown. "It's chilly at the beach. I...I was going to change when Palmer got here."

"Presumably because you want to look glamorous for your lover. When did you plan to put on makeup and fix your hair?"

She moistened her dry lips. "Why are you asking me all these questions?"

A smile relieved some of the strain on his face. "Your behavior is bizarre, even for a woman with limited experience at this sort of thing. You're supposed to curl up with Palmer, not a good book."

"I . . . they were to read till he arrived."

Garrett's mockery died. "What's going on, Kate? Why do you want me to believe this absurd fiction?"

She couldn't continue to stonewall. "I can't explain it to you. Just trust me," she said distractedly. "It has to be this way."

"Why don't you trust *me*?" he asked gently. "I can see you're frightened of something. Tell me what it is, sweetheart, and I'll take care of it."

"This time you can't." Tears streamed down her pale cheeks.

Garrett folded her in his arms and let Kate sob out her grief against his broad shoulder. When the torrent subsided he led her to the bed and sat beside her.

"All right, tell me what this is all about."

"You have to promise you'll go away afterward and leave me alone."

"You know that's impossible. I couldn't even stay away from you when I thought you were meeting another man."

"Oh, Garrett, you're making this so difficult."

"Tell me one thing. Do you love me?"

Tears welled up in her eyes again. "More than anything in the world."

"That's all that matters."

He enveloped her in a crushing hug and kissed her almost savagely. Kate clung to him with a kind of desperation, allowing herself one last brief moment of ecstasy. But when her hands moved feverishly over his straining muscles, Garrett drew back.

"You'll never know what I went through when I thought I'd lost you. Why did you put us through this purgatory, Kate?"

"There wasn't any other way," she whispered. "We can't get married, Garrett."

"The hell we can't! I'd like to see anyone try to stop us."

"Foster can't stop us, but he can ruin you. I love you too much to let that happen."

"What does Foster have to do with—" Garrett's eyes narrowed abruptly. "I'm beginning to get a clue. Did he come to you for money?"

"He made the most disgusting threats. You don't know what he's capable of! I couldn't let him do that to you, so I told him I wasn't going to see you anymore." The words came tumbling out almost incoherently.

Garrett held her hands tightly. "Take it easy, sweetheart. Just tell me what Foster said to you."

He listened in silence, his expression hardening as Kate related the sordid story. When she'd finished, Garrett swore pungently.

"Why didn't you come to me immediately?"

"Because I was afraid you'd insist on getting married."

"Darling Kate, do you really think I'd give you up?"

"You see what I mean?" she asked sadly. "One of us has to be sensible. Foster would destroy you out of pure spite."

"I doubt it, but it's a possibility." Garrett stood up and started to prowl around the room with a preoccupied expression.

"We can't take a chance," she insisted. "Surely you realize that."

"We're getting married," he answered almost absently. "This won't be easy for you, but you can do it."

"I'm not worried about myself!" she exclaimed. "How can I get through to you?"

"That's not what I meant, angel. I want you to do something distasteful. You're to call Foster and tell him you've changed your mind. You're ready to get the money for him.''

"I won't do it! He'd blackmail us for the rest of our lives.''

"Undoubtedly. But not after we take out a little insurance. You're going to get Foster's extortion attempt on tape.''

Kate looked at Garrett with dawning hope. "You think I could get him to incriminate himself? Would he really believe I'd trust him to keep his word?''

"You can be pretty convincing,'' Garrett replied wryly. "I have the emotional scars to prove it.''

"You couldn't have been any more miserable than I was.''

"You want to bet? We'll compare our wounds shortly. First I want to get all the details out of the way.''

They discussed Garrett's plan fully, where the microphone would go, what she would say to draw Foster out. When Garrett was sure Kate was thoroughly briefed, his businesslike manner changed subtly.

"Now that that's taken care of, we can move on to more important matters. Unless you still have some questions.''

"Just one.'' She unfastened her top button. "Do you really think this gown is unattractive?''

The glow in his eyes deepened as he watched her. "Can I see what my alternate choice would be?''

Kate lifted her gown slowly, prolonging the excitement that had begun to rage through her like wildfire. Garrett's smoldering gaze was almost unbearably erotic.

When she was completely nude he drew her between his knees and ran his palms over her body from shoulders to thighs. "This is how you appeared in my dreams. Don't ever leave me again, my love.''

"I couldn't." Her heart started to pound as Garrett's hands and mouth brought the special pleasure only he could create. "Love me, darling," she murmured.

"For the rest of our lives," he promised in a husky voice as he clasped her in his arms.

They didn't put their plan into operation until Monday night. Garrett had insisted they deserved the weekend together without any distractions, and it had indeed been a memorable one. In spite of her nervousness as she waited for Foster, Kate felt equal to any challenge.

She didn't try to conceal her loathing for him, since Garrett said that would appear normal. Foster did seem to expect hostility, and it didn't faze him.

"I thought you'd see things my way when you thought it over," he said.

"Is that the way it worked with your other blackmail victims?" she asked acidly.

"You insist on using that nasty word. I'm just a friend who's trying to do you a favor."

"For a price. That makes it extortion—if you prefer that word."

"I don't. All I did was ask for a loan. You had the option of refusing."

"In which case you'd spread lies about Garrett."

Foster was distracted momentarily. "You didn't tell him about this, did you?"

"Of course not. He'd never have given me the money."

He relaxed visibly. "Garrett isn't as realistic as we are. You did the right thing."

"I hope so. I don't like to think what he'd do if he ever found out."

"He won't. Where's the money?"

"Did you bring the photostat of my check?" she countered. When Foster produced it she said, "I want everything spelled out so there won't be any misunderstandings. If I give you twenty-five thousand dollars, you promise not to tell anyone that I hired your agency to get me a date. Is that correct?''

He smiled mockingly. "You're hurting my feelings. It sounds as if you don't trust me."

"Just tell me what I'm getting for my money," she answered grimly.

"Okay, if you insist. You're really making me work for it, but I suppose you're entitled. In exchange for a contribution to my legal fund, I'll refrain from discussing details of your life or my friend Garrett's."

That wasn't the proof she was seeking. Foster could slip out of the trap if she accepted his fiction that the money was a 'contribution.' But if she pressed too hard, he might become suspicious. Kate decided on a bold step.

"Forget it," she said. "The deal's off."

"What are you talking about? I told you what you wanted to hear."

"Not even close. You gave me a lot of double-talk. If I hand you one thin dime, you'll blackmail me from now on. I was crazy to think I could trust a two-bit hustler who would stoop to anything." Her mouth curled contemptuously.

"What the hell do you think *you* are?" he snarled, his temper rising. "You wouldn't be willing to pay blackmail if you weren't so wild to get your hands on Garrett's money. And you better pay it, baby, or I'll throw so much mud at your meal ticket that even *you* won't want him."

Garrett came strolling out of the bedroom. "I think that should do it," he said calmly. "Nice going, Kate."

Foster turned pale. "How long have you been in there?"

"Long enough to hear your confession. You're a great con man, Foster, but you're lousy at extortion. Maybe you'll pick up some pointers in prison."

Foster's eyes darted from Garrett to Kate and back. "You can't prove anything. I'll deny everything. It's my word against yours."

"Not quite." Garrett removed the flowers that concealed the tape recorder on the coffee table.

"That's entrapment!" Foster shouted.

"My, my, how fast you picked up the lingo. You should fit in well with the other cons. Pimping might be considered a misdemeanor, but extortion is a capital offense."

"You wouldn't do that to me," Foster pleaded. His face was ashen and he was shaking all over.

Garrett was unmoved. "You deserve worse for what you put Kate through."

"I'm sorry! I know it's no excuse, but I was desperate. If you'll just give me a break I won't ever bother either of you again. I swear to God!" Foster was babbling brokenly.

"Keep your word for once and I might reconsider," Garrett answered curtly.

After Foster had gone, Kate said tentatively, "You won't really press charges against him, will you?"

"No, but I wanted to shake him up so badly that he'd never try anything like this again."

"Will he go to jail on the other charge?"

"Considering that it's a first offense, I doubt it. He'll probably be slapped with a fine and ordered to put in some time doing community service."

"Is that fair to the community?" Kate asked dryly.

Garrett grinned. "Don't worry. I think Foster has seen the error of his ways." His smile faded. "I hope you have, too."

"What did *I* do?" she asked indignantly.

"You didn't come to me when he threatened you."

"I was afraid you'd insist on getting married anyway, in spite of the consequences. I couldn't let you make that great a sacrifice for me."

"Darling Kate. Don't you know life wouldn't have been worth living without you?"

"I found out what it was like without *you*," she answered in a muted voice. "You wouldn't believe what I went through when I thought I'd lost you forever."

"You should have known I couldn't stay away for long. This week has seemed like an eternity. Let's get married tomorrow," he said impulsively.

Kate was torn between desire and duty. "We have all kinds of arrangements to make first," she said doubtfully.

"I have the license and the ring. That's all we need—except each other."

Garrett was right, of course. Nothing was more important than the deep love they shared. She gave him a misty smile. "I can hardly wait for morning."

All the tension was gone from his face as he murmured, "We'll figure out a way to make the time pass quickly."

Kate smiled enchantingly as she twined her arms around his neck. "That's what I was counting on."

* * * * *

Take 4 bestselling love stories FREE

Plus get a FREE surprise gift!

PASSPORT TO ROMANCE
SWEEPSTAKES RULES

1. **HOW TO ENTER:** To enter, you must be the age of majority and complete the official entry form, or print your name, address, telephone number and age on a plain piece of paper and mail to: Passport to Romance, P.O. Box 9056, Buffalo, NY 14269-9056. No mechanically reproduced entries accepted.

2. All entries must be received by the CONTEST CLOSING DATE, DECEMBER 31, 1990 TO BE ELIGIBLE.

3. **THE PRIZES:** There will be ten (10) Grand Prizes awarded, each consisting of a choice of a trip for two people from the following list:
    i)   London, England (approximate retail value $5,050 U.S.)
    ii) England, Wales and Scotland (approximate retail value $6,400 U.S.)
    iii) Carribean Cruise (approximate retail value $7,300 U.S.)
    iv) Hawaii (approximate retail value $9,550 U.S.)
    v)   Greek Island Cruise in the Mediterranean (approximate retail value $12,250 U.S.)
    vi) France (approximate retail value $7,300 U.S.)

4. Any winner may choose to receive any trip or a cash alternative prize of $5,000.00 U.S. in lieu of the trip.

5. **GENERAL RULES:** Odds of winning depend on number of entries received.

6. A random draw will be made by Nielsen Promotion Services, an independent judging organization, on January 29, 1991, in Buffalo, NY, at 11:30 a.m. from all eligible entries received on or before the Contest Closing Date.

7. Any Canadian entrants who are selected must correctly answer a time-limited, mathematical skill-testing question in order to win.

8. Full contest rules may be obtained by sending a stamped, self-addressed envelope to: "Passport to Romance Rules Request", P.O. Box 9998, Saint John, New Brunswick, Canada E2L 4N4.

9. Quebec residents may submit any litigation respecting the conduct and awarding of a prize in this contest to the Régie des loteries et courses du Québec.

10. Payment of taxes other than air and hotel taxes is the sole responsibility of the winner.

11. Void where prohibited by law.

COUPON BOOKLET OFFER TERMS

To receive your Free travel-savings coupon booklets, complete the mail-in Offer Certificate on the preceeding page, including the necessary number of proofs-of-purchase, and mail to: Passport to Romance, P.O. Box 9057, Buffalo, NY 14269-9057. The coupon booklets include savings on travel-related products such as car rentals, hotels, cruises, flowers and restaurants. Some restrictions apply. The offer is available in the United States and Canada. Requests must be postmarked by January 25, 1991. Only proofs-of-purchase from specially marked "Passport to Romance" Harlequin® or Silhouette® books will be accepted. The offer certificate must accompany your request and may not be reproduced in any manner. Offer void where prohibited or restricted by law. LIMIT FOUR COUPON BOOKLETS PER NAME, FAMILY, GROUP, ORGANIZATION OR ADDRESS. Please allow up to 8 weeks after receipt of order for shipment. Enter quickly as quantities are limited. Unfulfilled mail-in offer requests will receive free Harlequin® or Silhouette® books (not previously available in retail stores), in quantities equal to the number of proofs-of-purchase required for Levels One to Four, as applicable.

PR-SWPS

OFFICIAL SWEEPSTAKES
ENTRY FORM

Complete and return this Entry Form immediately—the more Entry Forms you submit, the better
your chances of winning!
• Entry Forms must be received by **December 31, 1990**
• A random draw will take place on **January 29, 1991**
• Trip must be taken by **December 31, 1991**

3-SSE-1-SW

YES, I want to win a PASSPORT TO ROMANCE vacation for two! I understand the prize includes
round-trip air fare, accommodation and a daily spending allowance.

Name_____

Address_____

City_____ State_____ Zip_____

Telephone Number_____ Age_____

Return entries to: **PASSPORT TO ROMANCE**, P.O. Box 9056, Buffalo, NY 14269-9056

© 1990 Harlequin Enterprises Limited

COUPON BOOKLET/OFFER CERTIFICATE

Item	LEVEL ONE Booklet 1	LEVEL TWO Booklet 1 & 2	LEVEL THREE Booklet 1, 2 & 3	LEVEL FOUR Booklet 1, 2, 3 & 4
Booklet 1 = $100+	$100+	$100+	$100+	$100+
Booklet 2 = $200+		$200+	$200+	$200+
Booklet 3 = $300+			$300+	$300+
Booklet 4 = $400+	_____	_____	_____	$400+
Approximate Total Value of Savings	$100+	$300+	$600+	$1,000+
# of Proofs of Purchase Required	4	6	12	18
Check One	_____	_____	_____	_____

Name_____

Address_____

City_____ State_____ Zip_____

Return Offer Certificates to: **PASSPORT TO ROMANCE**, P.O. Box 9057, Buffalo, NY 14269-9057

Requests must be postmarked by **January 25, 1991**

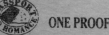

ONE PROOF OF PURCHASE

3-SSE-1

To collect your free coupon booklet you must include the necessary number of proofs-of-purchase
with a properly completed Offer Certificate

© 1990 Harlequin Enterprises Limited

See previous page for details